About the Author

Γ rn in Huyton, near Liverpool in 1957, T. K. Fairclough
ked as a safari park attendant and a door-to-door soft
ıks salesman before serving for 22 years in the Royal
Force and then afterwards as a security officer. He has
e adult children and two grand-daughters and lives in
cester. This is his first book.

For Mum, Dad and Hilda
1938 – 2016
Always in my heart and thoughts

T. K. Fairclough

THE GOLDEN IDOL

A Rick and Hugo Adventure

AUSTIN MACAULEY PUBLISHERS™
LONDON • CAMBRIDGE • NEW YORK • SHARJAH

A CIP catalogue record for this title is available from the British Library.

ISBN 9781788782258 (Paperback)
ISBN 9781788782265 (Hardback)
ISBN 9781788782272 (E-Book)
www.austinmacauley.com

First Published (2018)
Austin Macauley Publishers Ltd™
25 Canada Square
Canary Wharf
London
E14 5LQ

The Golden Idol is a work of fiction. All of the names, characters, organisations and events portrayed in this novel are either products of the author's imagination or are used fictitiously.

Acknowledgements

I would like to say a big thank you to the following people for the help, support and encouragement they gave me while writing the book and afterwards: Joanne Jones, Malcolm Dervan, Belinda Bennett, Anna Maria Rengo, Joanne Edmonds and Paul Smithson.

I should also like to give a special mention to the staff at Beaumont Leys Library for their technical help and to the staff of Greggs and Emma from Costa at the Beaumont Leys Shopping Centre for their good humour, excellent service and products.

Chapter One

I called them the usual suspects as they always sat in the café or got there just after; no matter what time I arrived. The café was in the middle of the central concourse, which formed part of the much larger Beaufort Shopping Centre, just outside of Leicester. The left-hand side was completely taken up by a supermarket and on the right was a collection of coffee, health food, bakers, newsagents, greetings card, shoe and mobile phone shops; brands that you would find on any high street. The ceiling was a glazed arch, through which I could see the clouds drift by in their slow, silent majesty across the bright-blue sky; and the warm sunshine felt good and reflected off the surface of the round metal tables.

A wizened old lady, who I would say was in her late sixties, with short white brushed back hair; the story of her life was written in the deep lines etched into her tanned, weather-beaten but kindly face. She would always be sat at her favourite table in the corner with a sausage roll and a cup of tea. No matter what the weather, she always wore a big black, hooded winter coat with voluminous green trousers. Tearing open the paper wrapper which encased the sausage roll, she would then lay it on top of the wrapper, take a bite, put it down and then fold her arms as she chewed on the hot snack. The cup of tea she would grasp with both gnarled hands, cherishing the warmth of the liquid inside as it radiated through the cup and warmed her hands, then she would take a sip and place the cup back

9

down to be replaced by another bite of the sausage roll. She would also appear at the Caffé Nero coffee shop I frequented in Leicester.

Next, was 'Dan the Man U Fan', as I liked to call him. He was in his fifties, of medium height and build, and always wore an expression like he was sucking on a Fisherman's Friend lozenge. Every day he was dressed in Manchester United Football Club apparel, from the red baseball cap with black-and-white trim on the peak and black padded jacket, to a pair of black tracksuit bottoms, all sporting the MUFC crest and Champions League logos. Nobody was left in any doubt of where his football team allegiance lay.

It would take him quite a bit of time to settle down at a table, he would leave his JD Sports carrier bag on a chair to say, "this table is taken" and then he would tidy away any used cups, food wrappers and paper napkins into the waste bin from his own table and would then go on to do the same at all the other empty tables, and then go and buy himself a cup of tea and a slice of pizza. He would return after a few minutes depending on the queue, with the tea and pizza slice, put them on the table and sit down after he had gotten four sachets of sugar, two wooden stirrers and some napkins from the wooden organiser that sat atop a wooden cabinet which housed the waste bin. After he had added the sugar and stirred his tea, he would pull out the triangular shaped hot pizza slice by its apex from the paper wrapper with the cardboard stiffener, with his thumb and forefinger, and then switch hands to feed the pizza into his mouth, but rather than raise the pizza to his mouth, he would lower his mouth onto the pizza and take a big mouthful. He struck up a conversation with me one afternoon when he saw I was reading a copy of *Flypast,* an aviation magazine, as he too had an interest in aircraft; it was then that he told me his name was Lionel.

Today, he had a can of paint with him, which he had placed on the table, and the fingers of his left hand rather annoyingly drummed rhythmically on the lid. I thought the tin said Prize Plum on the label, but as I craned my neck to see the rest of the label I noticed it actually read Sumptuous Plum!

The final suspect was an attractive looking mature woman with a large curly mane of unnaturally coloured red hair on which a pair of sunglasses was perched, together with lipstick and nails to match, and large silver earrings. The only other piece of jewellery she wore was a gold-coloured chain necklace with a gold letter "J' hanging from it, nestled just above her cleavage. I often speculated what the "J' stood for – Jane, Joyce, Joanna, Justine, Jasmine – the list was endless. She was elegantly dressed in an expensive looking knee-length black dress with a white continuous line all over, accessorised with a thin red leather belt, black fishnets and red high-heel shoes.

She would sit gossiping to her friend, who had her back to me; of whom all I can say had long brown hair and wore a cream coloured top. So intent on gossiping, the redhead's eyes, as if mesmerised, never left her friend's face when she was cutting up the food on her plate and eating, or adding sugar to her cup of tea and stirring it. It was as if her hands were guided by some unseen force. She caught me looking at her the other day, and as our eyes met, I gave her a cheeky wink and a smile, and she flashed me one of those Mona Lisa smiles that, although very nice, were very hard to interpret. I whittled it down to two options, either "get lost you saddo" or "come here you sexy beast", and while I was whittling, she had turned her attention back to her friend.

By the way, I'm Rick – Rick Shannon, seeker of adventure, the unexplained and the weird, and a big fan of Robert Ripley, the American author of the *Believe It or*

Not! comic strip. Staring sixty in the face, I'm six feet tall and carrying a few extra pounds with medium brown hair and a moustache, courtesy of 'Just for Men'.

I first became interested in the unexplained one evening when my father, brother and I were going to the local Labour Club for a night out. Beyond the wrought-iron gate of the front garden of my parent's home is a large flat field, a patch of green in an otherwise drab council estate. The field is bordered on all four sides, by houses, a school, a railway embankment and a golf course. When we left the house we all noticed a large horizontal rectangular shaped patch of the brightest, purest, white light on the field about ten metres away; I immediately strode quickly towards the light, while my brother Rod followed more slowly and was screaming at me to come back. I pressed on, despite his protests, and reached the light. I was just about to put my foot down inside the rectangular glow when it just disappeared, and the field was enveloped in an inky darkness. We both stood there stunned for a minute and then slowly walked back to our father who had remained by the front gate and was now shaking his head and looking at us both as if we had gone out. He explained to us that the light was from next door's toilet window which overlooked the field. Rod and I looked up at the small, vertical rectangle-shaped toilet window of our neighbours, the Dearlove's house and we both agreed that their toilet light could not have projected the rectangle of light we had seen, that far onto the field.

All that evening in the club, over our beers and the odd bag of cheese and onion crisps, Rod and I discussed the possibilities about what the rectangular-shaped light could have been – a star gate, an alien mother-ship, a gateway to another dimension or even a time machine, but what we both agreed on was that there was no way on this Earth that the light came from the Dearlove's toilet window, unless old man Dearlove had purchased an old Second World War, anti-aircraft searchlight from the classified pages of the *Liverpool Echo* and had set it up in the toilet, instead of a 60 Watt light bulb, and that our father knew far more than he was prepared to say.

Chapter Two

I always met Hugo on Friday afternoons at the café for a catch-up; hear about his latest exploits and our 'Fairy Cake Friday' ritual. Each Friday we would take it in turn to buy cakes to have with our coffee. One Friday, Hugo turned up with a Tesco 'Everyday Value' brand, chocolate and vanilla Swiss roll which he must have found in a dark corner of one of his kitchen cupboards or from behind the fridge. I would measure it with our home made 'Cake-o-Meter' which in reality was a white plastic ruler with 'Cake-o-Meter' written on it in black marker pen, and then cut the cake exactly in half with the ruler. When I pulled apart the two halves of the cake it was mouldy in the middle; Hugo took great pains to explain to me that this was because it was a green sponge! We drank our coffee in silence that afternoon.

Today, as it was my turn to buy the cakes and after scanning the triple chocolate muffins, custards, apple Danish, rock cakes, Belgian buns, jam doughnuts and yum yums on show in the glass-fronted cabinet, I settled on two pieces of spicy bread pudding or 'wet nelly' as some folk call it, and two large lattes.

"Afternoon Bert," Hugo boomed. Hugo always called me Bert, his ex-wife whose name was Melody was called Bertie, their five-year-old daughter Lauren was Baby Bert, the family cat Professor Plum was Furry Bert, and a large remote-controlled Dalek was named 'Bert the Dalek' that he had lost along with a water powered watch somewhere in his shed. Everybody else was simply called, Bert.

Hugo Twiss was in his mid-fifties, but told everyone he was only fourteen on account he was born on the 29 February and had the height and build of Moose Molloy from the Robert Mitchum, 1975 film version of *Farewell My Lovely,* and the face only a mother could love. He was completely bald with a large fleshy face, a flat nose with nostrils that his ex-wife described as being the size of a double-bay garage and had an inverted, triangular shaped tuft of hair in the crevice between his lower lip and chin. I thought he had the world weary look of Tony Hancock but he was big-hearted and when he laughed which was a lot, mainly at his own jokes, his whole face would light up; and he reminded me of a photograph I had seen in a history magazine of a character called 'Big Nims'; who was an African-American soldier in the American Expeditionary Force in France during the First World War, who was laughing out loud at an out of shot comrade trying on his gas mask for the first time.

Although he had left Birmingham decades ago, he still had a hint of a Brummie accent when he spoke. Hugo's alter ego was Max Fortune, a singer, comedian and impressionist on the pubs and clubs circuit in the Midlands. Hugo's, sorry, Max's burning ambition was to appear on the TV show *Britain's Got Talent.* He had been to many an audition over the years but had never been picked to appear before the celebrity judges.

I first met Hugo at a 'Mysterious Britain' convention held over a weekend in a hotel in Northampton several years ago and, after consuming copious amounts of beer, we found that we had a lot in common. In Hugo, I had found a fellow seeker and one who also shared my passion for coffee and cakes.

Today, Hugo had a beige baseball cap with 'NGK' in red letters on the front with the peak to the rear, parked on the back of his head and wore a black T-shirt with a picture on it of Doctor Leonard 'Bones' McCoy from *Star Trek* above the slogan 'Are you out of your Vulcan mind?!', a pair of faded, knee-length dark-blue shorts with huge cargo pockets on the thighs, the contents of which would have made even Ross Kemp wince, and a pair of brand new wheat-coloured Timberland boots completed his outfit. On his back was a large grubby looking black rucksack that he closely guarded and placed between his feet as he sat down at the table.

"Afternoon Hugo, how are you?" I asked.

"Oooh yes, I'm very well, thank you Bert," he said crossing his arms under his ample moobs and pushed them up. "I saw your Bert the other day at the bookies, and I didn't like the look of him. Well, neither do I but he's good to the kids," he said, then burst out laughing.

Although I had heard it several times before, it was still very funny every time Hugo did one of his Cissy and Ada sketches that were originally performed by Les Dawson and Roy Barraclough on the comedy sketch show *Sez Les*.

Hugo eyed the two sugar-topped, brown, rectangular slabs of bread pudding, "Ooh, I do like a nice bit of wet nelly," he said in one of his numerous comic voices and licked his lips with his long fleshy tongue, which Gene Simmons of the rock group Kiss would have been proud of, and then started the Fairy Cake Friday ritual.

"Is it Moody Monday?" Hugo asked.

To which I replied, "No."

"Is it Choosy Tuesday?"

"Err, no."

"Is it Weeiirrd Wednesday?"

"Definitely not!"

"Is it Thermidor Thursday?"

"I don't think so."

"Is it Fairy Cake Friday?" Hugo said.

"Yeessss!" we both cried in unison.

There was no need to use the Cake-o-Meter today as the cake did not need to be measured or cut and the final part of the ritual involved the handing over of the Cake-o-Meter like a baton to Hugo, to signify it was his turn next Friday to buy the cakes. With the ritual now complete, we then both tucked into the bread pudding, washing it down with the now warm latte.

I had noticed Hugo was being extra careful with his rucksack and reckoned that there must be something of value in it. I waited until Hugo had stopped chewing for a moment.

"What's in the rucksack, Hugo?" I asked, trying to make it sound offhand.

"Aaaaah…you'll like this Bert," Hugo replied with a smile.

This means trouble, I thought, but my interest was rising. Hugo reached down and picked up the large rucksack from between his feet with both hands and carefully placed it on the table-top and standing up, unzipped the main compartment and lifted out, again with both hands, something wrapped in a tatty but clean, dark-green hand towel and placed it on the table, returning the now empty rucksack to the floor. My eyes never lost sight of his hands as he began to carefully unfurl the towel from around the object inside, and as more of a gold coloured object became visible, I began to see a golden glow slowly spreading up Hugo's face like he was wearing a golden mask, and his eyes shone like the midday sun had risen in them. Finally, free from the towel, Hugo placed a small golden statuette gently onto the table.

"This is gold, Mr Bond; all my life I've been in love with its colour," Hugo pronounced in a German accent and sat down, chewing on another mouthful of bread pudding, waiting for me to say something.

Chapter Three

I sat there staring at the golden statuette. My mouth would have been wide open but for the fact it was full of bread pudding. I immediately recognised it as the golden idol from the opening sequence of the film *Raiders of the Lost Ark*. I played back the scene in my head, where archaeologist Indiana Jones battles all manner of obstacles in an ancient Peruvian temple to retrieve a golden Chachapoyen fertility idol. He then quickly replaces the idol on its weight sensitive altar with a bag of sand he judges to be the correct weight of the idol, and just as he thinks he's gotten away with the ruse, the booby-trapped altar triggers the temple to self-destruct. As Indy makes a dash to escape the crumbling temple with the idol, he is again confronted by all manner of obstacles including a giant rock ball and a treacherous local guide. When he finally exits the temple, he is forced to surrender the idol to rival archaeologist René Belloq at spear point by the indigenous Hovito tribe. Belloq then holds aloft the idol and as the tribesmen bow down to it, Indy seizes this moment to escape aboard a waiting floatplane.

I leant forward with my elbows resting on the table and with my fingers steepled in front of my face, and forced myself to swallow the last of the bread pudding so that I could speak.

"How much?" I said, nearly choking and having to drink some latte.

"How much what?" Hugo replied testily.

"How much did you pay for it on eBay?" I asked.

"eBay, eBay!" Hugo bellowed, looking and sounding incredulous. "This is no replica life size prop I bought off eBay, this is the real thing, Bert." Then in a more hushed tone, "It's...it's solid gold!"

I looked at Hugo and then at the statuette and repeated his words over and over in my mind. "*It's solid gold!*"

It was now my turn to look incredulous. I picked up the statuette off the table for a closer look. It was an ugly looking object and weighed, I guessed, slightly more than a bag of sugar and took the form of a kneeling female figure with an enlarged grinning head, and between her legs a baby is being born.

"So, what's the story with the golden idol, Hugo?"

Hugo took back the statuette and re-wrapped it in the green towel and carefully returned it to his rucksack, drained the last of his coffee, cleared his throat noisily and began his story.

"It all began when the director and producers of the film, organised a special party, for the actors and crew at some swanky hotel in Los Angeles in 1981. The interior of the hotel had been decorated like the interior of the temple from the film, and a solid gold idol had been specially commissioned as a centre piece and sat on a replica altar. Sometime in the early hours of the next morning when the last of the guests had left the party and the hotel staff began to clear up, one of them noticed the idol was missing. Guess what the cheeky thief or thieves had left in place of the golden idol, Bert?"

"Err...a bag of sand?" I said trying not to make it sound as if the answer was too obvious.

"How did you know?" Hugo said quizzically.

"Lucky guess," I replied, straight faced.

"Anyway," Hugo continued, "the police were called in and investigated the theft and it was widely covered by the media at the time, but no arrests were ever made and the idol was never recovered and the insurance company paid out."

"Okay, so how have *you* managed to end up with this solid gold statuette, Hugo?"

"A friend of a friend of a friend of a friend recommended me. It arrived this morning in a cardboard box by a motor bike courier who kept his helmet on which also had a tinted visor. I signed for it, then he left."

"Friends in low places, more like, to do what?"

"It's no big deal Bert, it's hardly the Maltese Falcon! I'm just acting as a courier to deliver the idol to some guy called the "Fatman" in London." Hugo emphasised the word by holding up his hands and making twitching 'rabbits ears' with his fingers.

"The Fatman!" I replied with more than a hint of disbelief. "Did the box have a tape recorder in it?"

"A tape recorder Bert?" Hugo queried.

"Good Morning, Mr Twiss, your mission should you choose to accept it, is to deliver the golden idol to our agent in London known only as the Fatman. As always should you or any of your team get caught or killed, the Home Secretary will disavow any knowledge of your actions. This tape will self-destruct in five seconds."

"Very funny Bert, very funny," Hugo replied, unamused.

I suddenly became aware over the piped music that played in the concourse, an increase in the level of chatter and activity going on beyond the tall, trough style wooden planters that housed various shrubs which acted as the forward boundary of the seating area of the café and the ice cream kiosk further on. I stood up to get a better view and the sound of the metal legs of my chair scraping across the floor alerted the other customers in the café to crane their necks in the same direction. To my amazement I saw what looked like Native Americans; some were bare headed with long black hair while others wore full feather war bonnets, and all were dressed in fringed buckskin tunics and leggings with multi-coloured beaded and tasselled chokers and breastplates. I was wondering what the hell was going on, and was beginning to think that somehow this had something to do with Hugo and his golden idol. I turned around to face him and was just about to speak when I heard the theme tune to *The Last of the Mohicans*, which was a pan flute standard. The film starred Daniel Day-Lewis as Hawkeye, the adopted son of a Mohican Chief. It was then I realised that the group of men were a pan flute band playing their haunting, traditional 'music of the mountains' together with all-time classics and today's pop songs, which were both soothing and relaxing. I sat back down in my chair, looking rather sheepish.

"Another coffee, Bert?" Hugo asked.

"Does Liz Taylor like wedding cake?"

"And there was me thinking it was diamond rings," said Hugo, laughing.

"Do you want another latte, Bert?"

"Err…no, I'll have a mocha for a change with chocolate sprinkled on top, thanks."

Hugo returned to the table with the coffees, and I waited for him to settle down.

"So, you were telling me about the Fatman."

"Yes, the Fatman is the name of my contact in London. I'm travelling to London on Sunday by train, staying overnight in a hotel and then on Monday handover the err, package and collect my fee, then return to Leicester in time for coffee and cakes. Easy peasy, lemon squeezy, Bert."

"Hmm, it sounds *too* easy Hugo," I replied.

"That's why I would like you to come with me, all expenses paid of course. You know you want to, Bert."

"Hmmm…it sounds very tempting, Hugo," I replied thinking it over. "Will there be adventure?"

"Definitely."

"Danger?"

"Probably."

"Femme fatales?"

"Hopefully."

"Okay, where do I sign?" I said resignedly. "I'm only coming to keep you out of mischief, even though the Austrian Grand Prix is on TV, this weekend."

"Brilliant, Bert!" Hugo balled his hand into a fist and extended it towards me. I did the same and as our fists made contact in a 'fist bump' we both made an explosion sound with our voices and then slowly pulled back our open, fully stretched out hands.

"I must be out of my Vulcan mind!"

"We're both out of our Vulcan minds, Bert!" Hugo replied, rubbing his hands together and smiling.

I looked across the café to where the redhead and her friend had been sitting. The friend had gone, and it looked like the redhead was getting ready to depart as well. She was looking into a compact mirror, pouting before applying more red lipstick to her full, sensual lips. Job done, she put the compact and lipstick into her designer black leather handbag, which had a small teddy bear pendant hanging by a chain from one of the handle brackets. Rising from her seat, she tugged down the bottom of her dress and walked over to where Hugo and I were sitting, her high heels click-clacking across the tiled stone floor.

"It's Julia," she said, standing beside our table.

"Pardon?" I replied, standing up, trying not to look too startled, but holding her gaze by looking directly into her soft hazel eyes and being seduced by the musky, unforgettable aroma of the Poison perfume she was wearing.

"You were wondering what the 'J' meant, it's Julia…Julia Delmonte."

Before I had a chance to reply, she kissed her well-manicured right index finger and then pressed it gently to my quivering lips. I felt as if I had just been tasered, as a surge of white hot electricity coursed through my body, and my scalp erupted in a mass of goose bumps. I stood there rooted to the spot, stunned, and then Julia flashed me another one of her enigmatic smiles, turned on her elegant heels and then sashayed off in the direction of the exit, but her erotic scent lingered like the ends of a rainbow. Hugo and I swapped startled looks. "I reckon you're in there, Bert."

"Hmmm," was all I could muster, feeling shaky as I sat down and waited for the cocktail of chemicals the encounter had triggered inside my body to subside. "Do you want another coffee?" Hugo said, sounding concerned.

"No thanks, Hugo, I need something stronger, let's go to the pub and have a proper drink and we can go over the plans for the weekend."

"Ooh yes," Hugo replied, without any hesitation.

Chapter Four

The Travellers Rest was on the edge of the shopping centre adjacent to the covered outdoor market, opposite McDonald's and a hop, skip and a zebra crossing away from the bus station. It was quite a modern and stylish design and wouldn't have looked out of place on a hilltop above the warm, turquoise coloured waters of the Mediterranean Sea. The low wall surrounding the front of the pub was full of drinkers enjoying the sunshine, as was the narrow seating area between the wall and the pub itself. We went in past the welcome sign and it was pleasantly cooler and darker than outside.

"What are you having, Bert?"

"Pint of bitter thanks." Hugo headed to the bar and I found us a quiet place to sit in the corner on the maroon coloured plush seats. The walls were covered in brown wallpaper with a white flowery pattern and the ceiling was painted cream with criss-crossing wooden beams from which hung brown lamp shades dotted with dead flies. Above my head hung a rectangular shaped mirror with an ornate heavy gold coloured frame, either side of which was a window with beige curtains tied back with rope and double wrought iron lamps with red shades which gave the place a homely feeling. From where I was sitting I had a good view of the large screen TV which had Sky Sports on.

Hugo set the drinks down on the dark brown rectangular table. "What's that you're drinking?" I asked.

"Strongbow Dark Fruit, it's cider mixed with blackcurrant and blackberry juice. Have a taste, Bert." I picked up his glass of the dark coloured liquid and drank a mouthful. "Mmm, quite fruity and refreshing. Talking of fruit, Hugo, whatever happened to that fruit soup concept you were working on?"

"Do you mean the 'You'll go cocker hoop over froot soop' concept?"

"Yeah that's the one, and wasn't there another one involving bread?"

"Rainbow Bread," Hugo laughed. "To make sandwiches more appealing for children to eat, I came up with the idea to have a loaf of bread with different coloured slices using natural colourants. I've just been too busy with one thing and another to pursue them."

"If the Muppets can pitch the idea of a giant crumpet to Mr Warburton, I'm sure you can pitch your 'rainbow bread' idea to him."

"I'll get around to it next year Bert." *Yes*, I thought, *the amount of stuff you've got to do next year will take the whole year to complete them.*

"So, what's the plan for this adventure of yours, Hugo?"

"Well, Bert," Hugo said leaning forward conspiratorially and speaking in a hushed tone, "I thought we'd meet up at Leicester train station at say, eleven o'clock on Sunday and then travel to London. Rooms are booked at a Travelodge a short walk away from the station. Then, on the Monday morning we walk back to the station and travel on the underground to Lambeth, from where it's a two-minute walk to the rendezvous point at ten o'clock. I then exchange the idol for cash with the Fatman, who will then facilitate the idol's handover to the freelance recovery agent in London, who will then negotiate a finder's fee with either the idol's owners or the insurance company."

"What do you know of this Fatman character?"

"Only that he's known in the trade for being completely reliable and trustworthy in his dealings, Bert."

"Sounds good to me," I said but privately I still had my reservations and thought it all sounded a bit *too* easy.

"I fancy something to eat now."

"Me too," replied Hugo. We both took a food menu out of the wooden holder and scanned through it. I was torn between the beef lasagne and the all-day breakfast, but after much internal discussion, I as usual, settled on the all-day breakfast. There was an XL version available where you got four of everything, but it sounded like a heart attack on a plate. After much reading and re-reading the menu, Hugo eventually settled on the steak and Marston ale pie with chips and peas. "Same again?"

"Cheers, Bert." I gathered up the empty glasses and headed to the bar, halting at the pool table temporarily, not wanting to interrupt while a brunette with a ponytail bent down to line up a shot, displaying a fair percentage of her bountiful breasts which were spilling out of her low-cut top. I watched as the ball was potted and then carried on to the bar.

The barmaid was a young girl, probably a student and had a severely cut jet-black bob with a green fringe. Her face was pale but pretty, and her 'cupid's bow' shaped lips glistened with black lipstick. Around her slim neck she had a narrow black choker about the thickness of a bootlace and wore a black T-shirt of the heavy metal band Slipknot; the design featured the band name in red and a shattered piece of glass which I assumed were the band's faces in the shards. On her right arm above the elbow was a very colourful tattoo. The part I could make out consisted of a black cat and a shamrock, but most of it was hidden under the sleeve.

"Yes, chick?"

"A pint of bitter, a dark fruit and a bag of cheese and onion crisps, please."

"John Smiths or Mansfield Smooth?"

"Oh err, Mansfield Smooth thanks, and can I order some food, please?"

"Yes, what's your table number?"

"Hugo, what's the table number?" I hollered over to him.

Hugo searched the table looking for the brass disc with the table number on it. "It hasn't got one!"

"Tell him it's on the food menu holder," the barmaid said, I repeated the instructions to Hugo.

"Oh right," he said and after a few seconds he shouted back 'four', and also held up four fingers.

"Table four, I'd like to order the all-day breakfast and the steak and ale pie, please." The barmaid fed the details into the till. "That'll be £16.30, chick." I paid her and returned to the table with the drinks and crisps.

"Did I tell you I won a competition on the radio, Bert?"

"No," I said, raising a curious eyebrow.

"Yes, I had to phone the radio station to claim my prize and an automated voice said, "To receive £25 please press 1 or to receive two tickets to an Elvis tribute night please press 2". Well Bert, I couldn't make up my mind whether to press 1 for the money or 2 for the show!"

I laughed out loud at Hugo's joke. "I thought you were being serious there for a minute. That reminds me, have you heard that song 'What Does The Fox Say?' It's really funny."

"Yes Bert, I really liked it."

"It was done by two Norwegian brothers who perform under the name of Ylvis."

"Elvis?"

"I knew you were going to say Elvis, Hugo. If you lose the 'E' and replace it with a 'Y', Ylvis. Well anyway, I went on YouTube in the library the other day and watched some of their other videos, the one called 'Stonehenge' is absolutely hilarious, also 'The Cabin' and 'Someone Like Me' are really funny too."

A young guy with short brown hair and wearing a short-sleeved, double fronted black chef's jacket with Mandarin collar and black trousers, brought the condiments box and the cutlery to the table and left without a word. I was pleased to see that the three squeezy bottles of mayonnaise, BBQ and red sauces were all made by Heinz and the brown sauce was a glass bottle of HP and not some supermarket own brand sauces. After a minute or two he returned carrying two plates of food.

"All-day breakfast?"

"That's me," I said. He then set my plate down in front of me and then the other plate in front of Hugo.

"Thanks," we both said. I was a little disappointed at the small amount of chips on the plate and squirted mayonnaise on them, and on the sausages, bacon, eggs and beans I poured on the brown sauce followed by a sprinkling of salt. Hugo was busy tucking into his pastry encased pie with gravy, chips and garden peas.

"Nice?" I enquired.

"Lovely, Bert, thanks, though I think they've overdone it with the peas." I looked at his plate and thought there were enough peas there for four people!

After several more drinks we left the pub and Hugo made his way to the bus station while I prepared to walk home. "See you Sunday, Hugo."

"Okay chief!" Hugo replied as I headed home laughing.

Chapter Five

I was very happy and looking forward to accompanying Hugo to London, but I couldn't help feeling that it was beginning to sound like another of his madcap misadventures, like the one a couple of months ago, when he had found in an Age UK charity shop in Leicester an original copy of the Beatles 1969 *Abbey Road* album, the cover of which featured the four band members walking across a zebra crossing outside the Abbey Road Studios in London. When he got home, he took out the record from the album sleeve to play on his music centre, and as he did so a piece of paper fell out onto the carpet. Intrigued, Hugo picked the paper up, and read with astonishment of the supposed death of Paul McCartney in 1966 and his replacement in the band by an imposter.

A rumour of the death of Paul McCartney had begun to circulate in September 1969, in a college newspaper in Des Moines, Iowa and was picked up by radio stations in Detroit and New York claiming that McCartney had left the EMI recording studios angry after an argument during a recording session and had crashed his car and died on 9 November 1966, and was replaced in the band by lookalike William Shears Campbell, better known as Billy Shears.

The remaining band members who had been coerced into the cover-up, left hidden clues of the deception for the fans to find in the imagery of the cover artwork, when certain songs were played backwards and in the interpretation of some of the lyrics in the albums *Abbey*

Road, Sgt Pepper's Lonely Hearts Club Band, Magical Mystery Tour and *The White Album*. Hundreds of clues have been found by fans known as 'cluesters'; these include the *Abbey Road* album cover, which supposedly features a funeral procession with John Lennon dressed in white as the clergyman, Ringo Starr dressed in black as the undertaker, Paul McCartney barefoot and out of step with the other band members as the corpse, and George Harrison dressed in denim as the gravedigger. In the background is a white VW Beetle with the registration LMW 281F, meaning that McCartney would have been 28 'if' he had lived. In the foreground of the *Sgt. Pepper* album cover there is a yellow wreath of hyacinths around a left-handed bass guitar. McCartney played bass guitar left-handed. Behind the image of McCartney, a hand is held up, a raised hand being a mystical symbol of death. A cloth arm patch which supposedly bears the initials 'OPD', which is police jargon for 'Officially Pronounced Dead', is worn on his blue 'Pepper' suit.

Most of the clues turned out to have simple explanations. The funeral procession, was just the band wearing their ordinary clothes and, as it was a hot day, McCartney didn't wear his shoes. The 'OPD' patch actually reads 'OPP' which stands for Ontario Provincial Police, which was given to McCartney while on a tour of Canada.

The rumours decreased after an interview with McCartney was published in *Life* magazine of 7 November 1969 at his secluded home, High Park Farm on the Mull of Kintyre. McCartney explained that after the break-up of the Beatles, he hadn't been in the press much, his public engagements had been few and he was spending a lot of time with his new wife Linda at the farm. The rumours surfaced again on 25 February 2015, using the anniversary of former Beatle George Harrison's birthday to publish a spoof exclusive interview in the *Hollywood Inquirer* with 74 year-old Ringo Starr, the only surviving member of the band. Afraid that the deception would never be revealed, Starr claimed the rumours that McCartney had died in a car crash in 1966 and was replaced by Billy Shears were true.

Hugo had made it his mission with the help of his fellow 'cluesters' around the country and abroad to try and find out the truth about the whole episode: if Paul McCartney, now Sir Paul McCartney, is still alive and to track down the elusive 'Billy Shears'. If McCartney did die in 1966 then Shears and the rest of the band had pulled off the biggest con trick in history.

Then there was the time he had gone to a Ufology Convention at a hotel in Coventry and had got talking to a guy called Joe in the bar who was selling VHS tapes of what he claimed was the 'real' Roswell autopsy film footage. The tale Joe told Hugo that evening over several beers and shorts began one evening in November 1941 over the night skies of Berlin, in Nazi Germany.

What had been assumed to be a British twin-engined medium bomber had been caught in the beam of a ground-based, radar-controlled searchlight and the two-man crew of a patrolling Messerschmitt Bf 110 night fighter closed in to intercept and shoot down the illuminated 'bomber'. When in range, the pilot opened fire with his nose mounted machine guns and cannons and the crew observed hits being scored on the upper surface of what they later described in their After Action Report as a 'shimmering flying disc' and moments later it flipped onto its back and plummeted to the ground.

The disc shaped craft was found two days later by a motorised reconnaissance patrol, half buried in some wasteland on the outskirts of the village of Beckberg, near Berlin, and the patrol commander had promptly reported the find to his superiors. Shortly afterwards a truckload of soldiers turned up to cordon off and guard the strange craft. After a few hours, an aircraft recovery tractor unit with trailer and a crane arrived and removed the craft to an unknown location. It was originally thought the downed craft had been a secret British aircraft but when the interior of the craft was inspected, three dead alien beings were discovered which were later subjected to a filmed autopsy and medical experiments before being disposed of.

Over the next few years, the Nazis developed their own flying disc alongside pilotless drones and rockets as part of their experimental 'wonder weapons' program, using the technology from the crashed alien craft and their own top scientists and engineers at a secret underground factory complex in Thuringia, Central Germany, where the first test flight had taken place in February 1945. With the end of the war a matter of months away, the whole program was relocated to a top-secret Nazi underground base in Antarctica, well out of reach of the advancing Anglo-American and Soviet forces, where the craft and many others became operational.

Fast forward to June 1947 and on a proving flight to the United States, a Nazi flying disc broke-up in mid-air and the debris fell over a large area of a ranch near the city of Roswell in south-eastern New Mexico. Ranch foreman, William 'Mack' Brazel of the J. B. Foster ranch had gathered up some of the debris of the flying disc he had found while checking his sheep during a thunderstorm, and had stored it for several weeks before eventually reporting it to Sheriff George Wilcox of the Chavez County Sheriff's Office who in turn notified Major Jesse Marcel, an intelligence officer with the 509th Bomb Group stationed at Roswell Army Air Field.

During the Second World War, the group flying Boeing B-29 Superfortress four-engined heavy bombers, had carried out the dropping of the atomic bombs on the

Japanese cities of Hiroshima and Nagasaki on the 6 and 9 August 1945, from their base on Tinian in the Mariana Islands.

Marcel, with agents Sheridan Cavitt and Lewis Rickett of the Counter Intelligence Corps, immediately set off to investigate the debris field in a staff car and while touring the area they came across a large piece of disc-shaped wreckage, found at the end of the trail of debris that extended for miles. Marcel and the two agents entered the interior of the wreckage and found the remains of three dead human bodies in helmets and flight suits still strapped in their seats at their flight control stations. The area was immediately closed off and every bit of debris and wreckage was recovered to Roswell Army Air Field and, after inspection was sent to the office of Brigadier General Roger Ramey, the Commanding General, 8th Air Force, part of Strategic Air Command at Fort Worth Army Air Field, Texas.

The three recovered dead bodies were sent to the base morgue where they were each subjected to a filmed autopsy by a team of military doctors, where it was discovered that they were all Luftwaffe aircrew personnel. The three crewmen were later identified as Oberstleutnant Wilhelm Richter, Hauptmann Jacob Lang and Hauptmann Karl-Heinz Vogel from an inspection of their identity discs, uniforms and insignia, which were worn beneath their specially adapted flight suits. Richter was recorded as wearing the Knights Cross of the Iron Cross with Oakleaves, which were often presented personally by Adolf Hitler. The fate of the bodies of the three crewmen after the autopsies and identification was not documented.

On the morning of 8 July 1947, Lieutenant Walter Haut, the Roswell public information officer issued a press release stating that personnel from the 509th Bomb Group had recovered a flying disc which had crashed on a farm near Roswell, which attracted a lot of media interest. Later that afternoon the press release was rescinded and the next day a second press release was issued stating that the 509th Bomb Group had mistakenly identified a weather balloon as the wreckage of a flying disc. The weather balloon story was itself a cover-up of a top-secret USAAF operation codenamed Project Mogul to detect Soviet nuclear testing, using specially equipped high- altitude balloons.

Chapter Six

The story faded after this until the late 1970s when renewed interest was sparked by conspiracy theorists and UFO enthusiasts, citing that the government had covered-up evidence that an alien spacecraft containing extra-terrestrial beings had crashed at Roswell in 1947. The powers that be in Washington declared that the real origins of the flying disc could never be disclosed to the general public and stated that "if these people want aliens, then we shall give them aliens!"

A plan was quickly concocted to make a short film of an alien autopsy using 1940's vintage film stock. An out of work movie director; famed for his aliens from outer space, along with other low-grade B-movies and some special effects technicians were hired to work on the project. This was the film that British entrepreneur Ray Santilli purchased from a 'retired military cameraman' in Miami, Florida in 1992, and was broadcast in the United States as a TV special hosted by *Star Trek: The Next Generation* actor Jonathon Frakes, by the Fox network as *Alien Autopsy: Fact or Fiction?* on 28 August 1995 and later worldwide.

The film became a media sensation and was broadcast repeatedly. Experts from all over the world were queuing up to either prove or disprove the film to be genuine or a hoax. The decision to make the fake film had been vindicated and while everybody and his dog's attention were focused on aliens, the true story of the Nazi crewed flying disc was hopefully buried.

In 2006 Santilli admitted that the film had been faked, but insisted that real footage of an alien autopsy had existed, but due to the deterioration of the original film footage he had been forced to recreate the film from memory. He was unaware he had made a fake of a fake.

The film of the autopsy of the three Luftwaffe crewman had come to light in 2012 but had been widely disregarded as a hoax by most people, who thought it was part of a government conspiracy to deny that aliens had crash-landed on earth in 1947, that one or more had been captured alive and that alien technology had been used to develop the US space program and a wide range of everyday objects.

The next morning after breakfast, Hugo, together with other like-minded people, accompanied Joe to an empty meeting room in the hotel which had a VCR player and they watched the footage of the autopsy for themselves; satisfied, all had happily handed over £30 each for a VHS video cassette.

* * *

Hugo's flat was on the first floor of a dark, eerie looking house with evergreen trees around the front entrance that were twice as tall as the house which contained six flats, three to each floor. The hallway and stairs were gloomy, and I climbed up carefully to the first floor and knocked on the brown wooden door of Number 13, which had a handwritten sign sellotaped to it saying, 'Postman please leave parcels on doorstep.' Hugo opened the door and I stepped into his world.

To say it was small was an understatement; it would have been known a few years ago as a bedsit, but was now marketed as a studio flat. The main room was painted magnolia with a red fitted carpet and had a large rectangular window at the far end, which looked out onto more trees where a pair of magpies flitted from branch to branch; beneath the window was a silver Casio MZ2000 electric piano keyboard which sat on an X-framed stand. Along the right-hand side was a bed, a cream and brown coloured night storage heater above which was a large-scale map of Great Britain blu-tacked to the wall with different coloured pins stuck in various locations, a red GPO Memphis modern but retro styled record, CD plus radio music centre and a large grey DVD cabinet filled to capacity with videos, DVDs and CDs. Along the left side was a door which led to the shower and toilet, two side-by-side bookcases so full of books, magazines and box files on unsolved murders and mysteries, that the shelves sagged in the middle. Above this was a row of five identical clocks; each had a white sticker at the bottom which bore the name of a city – Leicester, New York, Los Angeles, Tokyo and Moscow. On the end was another doorway which led to a small kitchen. Every horizontal surface was covered with bric-a-brac and *Doctor Who*, and *Star Wars* related toys and memorabilia. A worn black leather two-seat sofa, coffee table and large screen LCD TV on a stand completed the furniture. It looked like one big man cave and felt compact and cluttered, but comfortable.

We'd decided to make an event of watching the video tape. I had brought eight cans of Special Brew with me, and Hugo found a takeaway menu and telephoned the 'Emperor Ming' for Chinese takeaway and ordered king prawn curry with egg fried rice for me and beef chow mein for himself and a bag of chips for us both to share. While we waited for the food to arrive, we sat down to watch *Coronation Street* on the TV as Hugo was a big soap opera fan. I also had been a big fan of the soaps but had stopped watching them a while ago. I recently started to re-watch *Coronation Street* when Les Dennis joined the cast as former burglar Michael Rodwell. I was hoping to catch him answer a question he didn't know the answer to, in the style of ex-Corrie regular Mavis Riley with the phrase 'Well I don't really know' which he used to perform on the comedy sketch show *Russ Abbott's Madhouse*.

The food arrived about half an hour later and after Hugo had plated it up and found some cutlery we settled down in front of the TV to watch the video. Hugo took the video out of its plain black case, inserted it into the VCR and then pressed the play button on the remote control. We were both glued to the TV when it went all fuzzy and then an advert came on for a cut-price airline, offering cheap flights from Birmingham to Alicante, then the picture changed to a bus depot and a long-legged and short-skirted clippie was changing the route number on a bus with the driver and conductor looking on.

"This is the *On the Buses* film," I said to Hugo. Hugo pressed the fast forward button and after a few seconds, pressed play again and the scene changed to a bus being driven along the road with the opening titles of the film and the theme tune, 'It's A Great Life On The Buses' being played. Hugo then pressed fast forward again for longer this time and then pressed play again and the scene showed members of the Butler household sitting around the dining table having a meal, when a new washing machine arrives. Hugo pressed the eject button on his remote control, bent forward and removed the video from the VCR and looked at the label curiously and then looked through the stack of videos in his cabinet, reading the labels, thinking he may have selected the wrong video.

"I don't understand it," he said, looking totally mystified and shaking his head.

"Have you watched the tape since you returned from the convention?"

"Yes, twice!" Hugo shrilled.

"Then you've taped over it with the *On the Buses* film. I was really looking forward to watching the video!" I replied.

Hugo sat there with a thousand-yard stare on his face, contemplating how he had managed to tape over the video he had bought at the convention. Then all of a sudden, he was on his feet, reaching into his coat which was hanging on the hook behind the front door and pulled out his wallet. He rifled through all the bits of paper and business cards in it until he found the one he wanted and then picked up his mobile phone from the coffee table and dialled the number on the card. Hugo's face dropped like shares on 'Black Wednesday' as he passed me the phone. I listened as the recorded female voice repeated, "The number you have called is not recognised, please check the number." I then took the card from Hugo's quivering fingers and read it; "Joe Noone, Ufologist," and then his mobile number with a comic representation of an alien's head on it. I handed the card back to Hugo who was still stunned by his carelessness.

"Interesting name that is, Noone."

"Interesting how?" Hugo replied, staring intently at the card.

"Well, it looks to me like if you put a space between the two o's of Noone it reads as No one, Joe No One. This is a man who doesn't want to be found." Hugo looked at the card again, shook his head and put it back into his wallet.

"Fffff...flipping heck! Well that's that then, drat, drat and double drat!" Hugo said resignedly.

I put a reassuring arm on his shoulder. "C'mon Hugo, why don't we have another beer, finish eating our Chinese and watch the *On the Buses* film *you've* so kindly recorded."

"Ooh yes," said Hugo in one of his comical voices, a smile returning to his lugubrious face.

Chapter Seven

As agreed, I travelled by bus to meet Hugo at Leicester train station on Sunday morning at 11:00 and, as the bus neared the station I saw him out of the window, admiring the Thomas Cook bronze statue which stood just outside the station. The statue of the founder of the world-famous travel agency of the same name, bags packed with an umbrella and holding either a pocket watch or a compass, had been unveiled in 1991 to commemorate the 150th anniversary of his first excursion by train, escorting temperance campaigners from Leicester to a rally at Market Harborough in 1841.

I got off the bus at the stop just past the station and walked back to meet him. If Hugo was trying to look inconspicuous, he had failed miserably. He was wearing a black fedora with a hatband that simulated a piano keyboard, a pair of Rayzor wraparound sunglasses, a long, black Western-style duster coat that covered a pair of black trousers and a pair of black leather three buckle boots; he looked like a mash-up between Elwood Blues and Wyatt Earp.

"Morning, Hugo."

"Morning, Bert." Hugo then took off his fedora and handed it to me and from his coat pocket produced what looked like a brown leather flying helmet with attached goggles and pulled it onto his head. "*Weeeee, tsk-tsk-tsk, bub-bub-bub-bub-bub, bulla-bulla,* pepper in the pigeon and when *he ahh-choooo, aww, ahh, pow*, the missile we *wipp-wipp-wooooh*, in on him and then *rip bang ballcock boom*, no more pigeon! What did he say? What did he say? H-he s-says r-ready t-to c-catch t-the p-pigeon, c-chief." We both fell about laughing at Hugo's impressions of the characters of the Vulture Squadron from the classic cartoon *Catch the Pigeon.* We walked, still laughing the few yards to the station.

Leicester train station dominates the stretch of London Road between Station Street and Conduit Street and is the only one remaining of Leicester's seven train stations, and replaced the earlier Campbell Street Station, which had been Leicester's first mainline station and was built on the site of the current station in 1840. By the 1880s it was no longer suitable to cope with the increasing levels of passenger and parcel traffic and the station was completely rebuilt and opened in 1892 and was renamed Leicester London Road. On one of my many walkabouts around Leicester, like Thomas Cook's Leicester and King Richard III Walking Trails, using leaflets available at the Visit Leicester.info shop, I came across the pair of stone gate posts at the end of Station Street, which is all that remains of Leicester's first mainline station.

The interior of the station was ultra-modern, but it still retained the grand Victorian red-brick and stone front facade with its historic turret shaped clock tower, being the only hand-wound station clock in the country and four archways. The left-hand pair were inscribed 'Departure' and the right-hand pair 'Arrival' and were designed to assist the horse drawn Hansom cab drivers in dropping off passengers to catch trains and picking up passengers on arriving at Leicester.

Hugo headed to the ticket office to buy the train tickets and check the train times, while I headed to the Gourmet Coffee Bar & Kitchen to buy the coffees.

"Two large mochas please," I said to the young girl behind the counter. Her long black hair was plaited into a ponytail which rested on her left shoulder.

"Any chocolate sprinkles?"

"Yes, please."

"Anything else?"

"No thanks."

"£5.70…sorry did you say chocolate sprinkles, or not?"

"Yes, chocolate sprinkles, thanks. Long day?"

"Long morning," she said, yawning.

I sat at one of the round wooden-topped tables with the metal silver and blue chairs and began to flick through the copy of the *NME* that had been left on the table. The cover featured two laughing girls rolling around in the mud at the Glastonbury Festival.

Hugo returned with the train tickets, gave me one and sat down at the table. "There's a train at twenty-two minutes past twelve, Bert."

I looked at my mobile phone as I did not wear a watch. It wasn't one of those all singing and dancing phones, it just sent and received calls, texts and photos, which was good enough for me. "Plenty of time Hugo. They do home-made porridge pots here, if you fancy one."

"I was ravenous when I woke up this morning, Bert, so I had a full English breakfast at the caff before I caught the bus."

"I didn't know the café was open on Sundays."

"Yes, only until one o'clock, though. What about you, Bert?"

"While I was waiting for the 54 bus, I went to McDonald's and had a double sausage and egg McMuffin, two hash browns and an orange juice, so I'm all right for now. I'll feel hungry again, though, by the time we get to London."

"Me too."

"Where did you get that crazy hat?"

"From the market...do you want me to get you one?"

"Let me think about that for a moment errr...no thanks! It's not exactly discreet, is it?"

"Don't you like it?"

"Yes, it looks very good on *you,* but I'd have thought we didn't want to attract any unwanted attention to ourselves, if you know what I mean."

"Relax, Bert, we're just two guys travelling to London for a few days of fun." *Relax!* I thought, *I'm riding shotgun to a solid gold statuette and he tells me to relax!*

"What did you do yesterday, Bert?" Hugo said, breaking my thoughts.

"I fancied a bit of a change and decided to go to Loughborough for the day. Have you ever been?"

"No, I haven't actually, Bert."

"I've only been once before and that was by car. From the bus station you have to get on one of those little Centrebus buses and it goes along all these winding country lanes through the rolling countryside of rural Leicestershire, passing along the way joggers, ramblers and cyclists and little villages like Cropston, Swithland and Quorn, and there's some very nice-looking pubs along the way. The bus drops you off in the centre of town right next to the market. On Saturday, though, it's mainly food and clothing. We will have to go one Friday and have our 'Fairy Cake Friday' there, as that's when they have their flea markets on."

"That's a good idea, Bert, I love roaming around flea markets, me."

"And me. I had a really good all-day breakfast in a nice café that mainly sources its food locally and also makes hand-made cakes, and then I had a look around the shops. There's loads of charity shops and I bought a book on motor racing and one that would interest you – *The*

Ultimate TV Guide, which is packed full of info on programmes from 1946 to 1999."

"You'll have to let me borrow it."

"I will. Then in the evening I did some ironing, packed my bag ready for the morning and then watched a few episodes of the final series of *Blake's 7* on DVD. What did you get up to?"

"Pretty much the same as you, actually. I went to the caff and had my usual full English breakfast, then I went into Leicester and had a look around the markets and charity shops."

"Did you buy anything?"

"No, there was nothing that really took my fancy. Then in the afternoon I started my first shift in the launderette I told you about, the 'Wash 'n' Go'."

"Yes, I remember you telling me about it, how'd it go?"

"It's all right, actually, I just have to sit there from three until seven pm, three days a week, giving out change for the machines and selling cups of washing powder and tea and coffee to the customers."

"Sounds like a nice little number, Hugo."

"Yes, it's not bad actually."

"I will have to start calling you Dot."

"Dot?" Hugo said, sounding puzzled.

"Dot Cotton."

"Cheers, Mr Opodopoulas," Hugo said, laughing. "Then in the evening I just watched TV."

Chapter Eight

Hugo looked at his watch. "It's five past twelve, Bert, we'd better make a move." We got up, grabbed our bags and walked into the station concourse. On the left was a W.H. Smith shop and, I was about to tell Hugo I was popping inside but he had marched briskly off, so I abandoned the idea and caught him up. We went through the ticket barriers and walked along the enclosed footbridge to the far end and went down the steps onto Platform 3.

Walking along the platform, I came across another W.H. Smith. "I'm just popping into Smith's", I shouted, but he had wandered off along the platform. I went through the open doors and perused the racks of magazines and settled on the *2000AD* Sci-Fi Special comic and then grabbed a bottle of water from the chilled cabinet. I paid for the comic and water and then quickly joined Hugo out on the platform, he was sitting on the grey metal seats outside the Pumpkin Café shop holding two large cups of coffee. "For the journey, Bert."

"Thanks Hugo." I took the coffee and sat down beside him.

"The next train to arrive on Platform 3 will be the 12:22 East Midlands Trains service for London St. Pancras only. This train is formed of five coaches. First class accommodation is towards the front of the train," a female voice announced over the Tannoy. A few minutes later, a yellow, red and blue painted train nosed into the station. We both got up, walked forward and stood behind the yellow safety line and had judged where to stand on the platform spot on, as we were right in front of a carriage door when the train came to a halt.

After a minute, the red door slid open and, after letting the passengers off, we climbed aboard, and I was surprised to see that the carriage was virtually empty, and walking along the aisle, I chose some seats with a table which didn't have any reserved tickets in the slots in the top of the seat backs. We sat down opposite each other in the seats nearest the aisle, with my back facing the direction of travel, which I didn't mind, but some nesh folk like Hugo *have* to sit facing forward. The interior of the carriage was cream-coloured with red seats and had a blue carpet with irregular red and yellow splotches. A double blow on a whistle sounded from the platform and the train eased out of Leicester.

"Did you ever fancy any of the Angel pilots from *Captain Scarlet and the Mysterons*?"

"Fancy them, I married one, Bert!"

"Oh, very droll Hugo, by the way, how is Melody?" I enquired.

"Yes, she's okay, both her and Baby Bert are off to the Algarve next week with her new boyfriend, Derek."

"Very nice. Are you seeing anybody else?"

"Not really but there's a woman called Ruth who works in the chippy that keeps giving me the eye and always gives me far more chips than the other customers and sometimes slips in an extra sausage."

"The 'Chish & Fips' chippy?"

"No, the 'Batter Me Up'. She's the slim one with the straight hair and curly teeth!"

"Don't you mean curly hair and straight teeth?"

"No Bert," Hugo said, straight-faced. I smiled on the inside.

"She won't stay slim long, working at the chippy."

"I know, that's what worries me, Bert," We both laughed.

"Do they still sell those jars of cockles in chippies now?"

"They used to, but I haven't seen them for ages, it's all pickled eggs, onions and gherkins now. I used to love a garlic and chilli cockle sandwich."

"A cockle sandwich!" I said, astonished.

"Yes, Bert, they're delicious, but they taste even better on laver bread. What were the Angels' names again?"

"Oh, err…Melody, of course, Harmony, Symphony, Rhapsody… I can't think of the fifth one's name now."

"Was it Cacophony?"

"Cacophony!" I laughed. "Would you seriously go out with someone called Cacophony?"

"Well, probably not, but she sure would make a hell of a lot of noise!" We both chuckled.

"That's gonna bug me for the rest of the day now, the name of the fifth Angel," I said.

"What was the name of the Chinese one?"

"Harmony."

"That figures, that's the one I liked. Which one did you like, Bert?"

"The red head, Rhapsody."

"I think you've got a thing about redheads, Bert."

"I have," I mused, thinking of Julia.

I looked up the carriage and watched the other people on the train, sleeping, chatting on mobile phones, drinking and reading newspapers and the latest paperbacks; one man, I had to smile, was reading *The Silver Locomotive Mystery* in Edward Marston's the Railway Detective series of books. I had read a few of the author's books set during the Duke of Marlborough's campaigns in the War of the Spanish Succession, but was disappointed that the paperback covers depicted British soldiers wearing uniforms from the Napoleonic era, one hundred years later!

It was then, I noticed there was a guy sitting a few seats up from us on the opposite side that I was sure I had also seen in the Traveller's Rest on Friday night. I had first noticed him standing on the platform at Leicester talking on his mobile phone, but couldn't place his face at the time. He was thirty-something, lean and had a plain cheerless face that had a hint of a moustache, and brown hair that was worn long on the top and short at the back and sides. A mirror lensed pair of sunglasses sat on the top of his head and he wore a grey short-sleeved shirt with blue jeans and white trainers. He sat flicking through a copy of the *Angling Times* while taking occasional sips from a tall can of Monster energy drink. He had an aura like his shirt, that nobody would give a second glance to.

"Don't turn around Hugo," I said in a hushed voice. "It might be just a coincidence but behind you, a few seats up on the right-hand side, there's a guy in a grey shirt sitting on his own that I am ninety-nine per cent positive I saw in the pub on Friday, and now he is sitting in the same carriage as us. I want you to go to the toilet and see if you recognise him on the way past."

"I need to go to the toilet, anyway, with all that coffee." Hugo got up from his seat and passed the guy on the way to the toilet.

After a good fifteen minutes, Hugo returned to his seat. "What kept you?"

"I really *did* need to go to the toilet, Bert."

"And the guy Hugo?" I said impatiently.

"Oh yes, sorry, I saw him in the pub too."

"Then we have to assume that we really do have someone tailing us. The big question is, which one of the following three options is he tailing us for?" I counted them off on my fingers. "One, that he will at some point attempt to snatch the idol; two, to make sure nobody else snatches the idol before we deliver it to the Fatman and three, to ensure that *we* don't do a runner with the idol. What do you think?"

"Yes, I agree with you, Bert, but the only one I think we have to worry about really is the first option, if he makes an attempt to snatch the idol."

"I agree. He's not aware as far as I know that we've spotted him, so let's keep it that way and keep our eyes peeled for him at all times, and if you can keep at least one arm looped around one of the rucksack straps at all times in the event he does try to snatch the idol and do a runner."

"Understood," Hugo said, looping his arm through the left strap.

"Do you fancy some space food, Bert, to keep you going until we get to London?" Hugo unzipped his rucksack and pulled out two small foil pouches.

"Space food?" I queried as I drained my coffee cup.

"Yes, you can buy it on the internet, and outdoors or camping shops. They used to sell it in Hawkins Bazaar and I suppose the National Space Centre would have it on sale in their shop too." Hugo then passed me one of the foil pouches; on the front was a photograph of an astronaut with the writing 'Freeze-Dried Ready to Eat Space Food' and then underneath 'Astronaut Neapolitan Ice Cream'.

"Thanks, Hugo," I said, and then tore open the pouch. Inside was about a two and a half-inch square by a half-inch thick, brown, white and pink block. It was very light and brittle and the Neapolitan ice cream flavours of chocolate, vanilla and strawberry just melted in the mouth. Don't get me wrong it was very nice, but if I was an astronaut I wouldn't want freeze-dried ice cream, I would want freeze-dried New York cheese cake or freeze-dried blueberry muffins, which I could eat all day long. In space, no one can hear you eat Neapolitan ice cream!

Chapter Nine

The train rattled along at a brisk pace towards London. I expected to hear the classic *da-duff, da-duff* sound as it passed over the railway tracks, but there was just a low chugging sound from the diesel engine above which the passengers chatted, and the sound of the push button automatic inter-carriage doors rumbling every time they opened and closed as people went to and from the toilets.

"Any more tickets, please," said a female voice from behind me. The train conductor was slim with shortish brown hair with blonde highlights and fashionable glasses and wore a smart dark-blue suit, light-blue blouse with a red cravat and a name badge that read, Dawn. We gave her our tickets and she scribbled on them in biro, returned them and then proceeded to the next occupied seats.

I looked out of the window to see the lush green countryside sweep by, interspersed with pockets of civilisation; fields were of different colours of green bordered by darker coloured hedgerows and trees, electricity pylons and telegraph poles ran parallel to, or criss-crossed the track taking power and communications across the land. Church spires rose in the distance like they were pointing to the heavens through the blue sky.

The sound of the drinks and snacks trolley trundling along the aisle brought my attention back inside the carriage. The operator was a young man with short black hair and he was wearing a grey waistcoat and matching trousers, a lilac shirt that looked like he had put it on straight out of the packet, as it was full of creases, and a red and blue striped tie. He wore a white name badge on his chest which read Viliam. "Fancy a coffee, Bert?"

"No thanks, I've got a bottle of water to keep me going, I'll wait until we get to London for a coffee."

"Me too, I think." The trolley trundled on down the aisle.

I looked at my mobile phone to see the time, it was 13:10 and then I looked out of the window just in time to see a station flash by, but the train was travelling too fast for me to catch the name. The trolley man reappeared, this time clutching a green bin bag, and he collected all the empty cups, food wrappers and discarded newspapers from the tables and seats. Then along came the conductor to collect all the reserved tickets from the back of the seats.

The train showed no sign of slowing down but the passengers were getting themselves ready to leave, packing their stuff away in bags, rucksacks, brief cases and laptop bags, while ladies touched up their make-up, putting on coats and jackets and making their way to an exit. I looked at my mobile phone again, it was 13:44, a good ten minutes before we were due to arrive in London. I couldn't see the point of standing, waiting to get off, so we remained in our seats.

"Do you remember the *Lone Ranger* series with Clayton Moore, Bert?"

"Yes, of course, it was on every Sunday night, if I remember rightly. I loved it."

"Can you remember the name of the guy who played Tonto?"

"Everybody knows that…Jay Silverheels," I replied confidently.

"Ah, but did you know his real name was Harold Smith?"

"Harold Smith! I never knew that, it doesn't conjure up the image of a Native American does it? I just took it that his real name was Jay Silverheels."

"Yes, Harold Smith, he was the son of Canadian Mohawk Chief George Smith. And did you also know that the Green Hornet was a relation of the Lone Ranger?"

"Yes, I knew about the connection to the Green Hornet. Are you practising for Eggheads or something?"

"Maybe, maybe not," Hugo replied with a grin.

"I used to call one of my ex-girlfriends The Lone Ranger," I said.

"Oh, why was that, Bert?"

"Because she was always going through my pockets looking for Silver!"

"Good one," Hugo said with a guffaw.

A barely audible voice came over the Tannoy, I guessed welcoming us to London St. Pancras International. The train slowly pulled into the station and came to a halt with a judder. We remained in our seats until we found a gap to join the queue to leave the train. I stole a glance at the guy in the grey shirt who was busy putting on a dark-blue jacket. We eventually got off and, dodging between the two-wheeled luggage trolleys that half the passengers hauled behind them, walked along the platform passing along the first class carriages and the train engine on the right, which bore the name *The Flying Foxes,* and on the left were some Eurostar liveried trains as we queued to go through the ticket barriers which kept our tickets.

St. Pancras International was a marvel of Victorian engineering but I thought it looked like an enormous aircraft hangar rather than a cathedral as others might describe its magnificence. The sky-blue painted wrought-iron girders, arranged in a lattice framework, supported a glazed arched roof running along the centre. At the far end, at the apex of the iron archways hung the station clock; a huge Dent white-faced clock with gold leaf hands, border, and Roman numerals which were set in slate diamond shapes. I glanced around, hoping to catch sight of the guy in the grey shirt, but couldn't see him anywhere in the crowd but I was happy to see that Hugo had chosen to wear the rucksack with both arms through the straps.

We went down the escalator and came into a shopping arcade that had high end brand name shops on either side with floor-to-ceiling glazing: Pink, L'Occitaine, Fat Face, Joules, Hamley's, Godiva, Fortnum & Mason to name a few together with the obligatory W.H. Smith and currency exchange shops, it was just like being at Heathrow Airport.

Walking along the row of shops bustling with people, we came across a brown piano beneath a set of steps that led to the upper concourse level above. On the open lid it said, 'Play Me, I'm Yours'. This invitation was like a red rag to Hugo as the entertainer in him came out. He removed his rucksack from his back and passed it to me to mind as he promptly sat down on the wooden stool, pretending to flick out his coat tails. He then held out his interlocked hands in front of him and flexed them, cracking his knuckles, and then tickled the ivories like the professional he was. He played the theme tune from the *Eastenders* TV series and before long, a crowd of people had gathered around the piano with some taking photos and filming Hugo on their cameras and mobile phones.

While Hugo continued to entertain the crowd, I continued to glance around hoping to see if I could spot our mystery 'friend' milling around in the crowds of people, but he was nowhere to be seen, but I had a funny feeling he was watching us. Hugo finished with a *dee da-da dee-dee...dee-dee*! He then got up and took a bow while the crowd and I clapped for his impromptu performance followed by more photographs.

"Come on, Liberace," I said, as we continued walking along the arcade and found the toilets. As both of us needed to go, we took it in turn to use them, while the other looked after the bags. The toilets were free to use and in common with most toilets everywhere there was a long line of women queuing to use the Ladies. Job done, we looked around for an exit, but there were so many in the station to choose from that we decided to ask someone for directions onto King's Cross Road. "There's a policeman over there, we can ask him."

"Well spotted, Bert."

"Excuse me, can you tell me which is the best exit to take for King's Cross Road, please?" I asked.

The officer held out his right hand. "If you take this one on the right and then turn right out of the station, follow the Great Northern Hotel around to the left and then turn left."

"Thank you," I replied. As we walked past the Eurostar international departures terminus to Paris and Brussels to exit the station through the glass doors. I couldn't help thinking that the French must feel a whole lot better arriving at King's Cross rather than the previous Eurostar station at Waterloo!

Chapter Ten

Outside the station we crossed a road with lots of taxi traffic and turned right, walking between the Great Northern Hotel bar which had red metal tables and chairs outside covered in red-and-white checked table cloths, and a Pret A Manger sandwich shop. We found ourselves unexpectedly in the large open space of King's Cross Square where, to our left, there sat an unusual shaped sculpture. Hugo wanted to see what it was, so we walked over to it. On the circular base was a plaque to say that the bronze sculpture was called *Large Spindle Piece* by Henry Moore. The form of the sculpture left me at a loss if ever I had to explain it to someone else who had never seen it before, as it was very open to interpretation, but I thought it had a sense of motion about it. I ran my hand over it and though it was cold to the touch, it felt very tactile, and then to get away with trying to explain it, I took some photos of it on my mobile phone.

We sat down on one of the granite benches which were shaded by a row of London plane trees. Sitting across the front of the piazza-like square, which had stripes of light and dark-grey granite, was the restored yellow brick frontage of King's Cross station. It displayed none of the Victorian extravagance of such places and was rather plain and functional looking. It had a glazed arch on either side of a central, tall clock tower. I opened up my holdall and took out my bottle of water. "Water, Hugo?" I asked, offering him the bottle.

"No thanks, Bert, I've got some water." I unscrewed the lid and took a long slug, closed my eyes, and tossed my head back and soaked up the warmth of the sun.

"C'mon sleepy head," said Hugo, standing up.

"I was just resting my eyes," I replied, and then reluctantly got to my feet and swigged the remainder of the water. I looked around to find a litter bin but there didn't seem to be any, so I returned the empty bottle to my holdall.

Across the other side of the road, I spied a Ladbrokes betting shop which had a sign above it saying, 'Euston Road' and looking around saw no sign of King's Cross Road. To the right was the historic clock tower of the St. Pancras Renaissance Hotel.

"Aww Gawd, you've gone and done it this time, Butler," Hugo said, rocking backwards and forwards on his feet and flapping his arms by his sides like a penguin. We both burst out laughing and after looking around again, we turned left as the policeman had said, and walked along Euston Road and crossed over the very busy York Way and on into Pentonville Road, hoping we were going in the right direction.

"It must be further down," I said to Hugo.

"It's just like walking along a real game of Monopoly, Bert."

"It does a bit," I replied.

We walked on and passed Gray's Inn Road on the right.

"Let's stop at this Starbucks that doesn't look too busy, Bert, and have a coffee and something to eat."

"Yes, I'm feeling quite peckish now." We went in and Hugo went to the counter while I found us some seats.

"Do you want brown sauce or ketchup, Bert?" Hugo shouted over his shoulder.

"Always brown," I shouted back. After a few minutes Hugo placed a tray on the table with two rolls and two medium waxed paper cups of latte on it. Hugo handed me one of the hot rolls on a plate with two sachets of brown sauce. "I got us an all-day breakfast roll each to keep us going, Bert."

"Cheers, Hugo," I said lifting off the top of the roll to find that it had scrambled egg, bacon, and sausage inside, to which I added both sachets of the sauce eventually; having failed to tear them open with my hands, I had to resort to using my teeth. I noticed both cups of coffee had our names on them in black marker pen. My cup, not surprisingly, was marked with 'Bert'.

"What's with the names on the cups, Hugo?"

"I suppose they have to, so they don't get confused with the number of customers." I looked around the café and counted five other people with us making seven.

"Yes, very confusing, Hugo," I replied.

At the next table sat a young woman with short brown hair tucked behind her ears, who was furiously scribbling away with a blue topped pen in an A4 sized exercise book with a red cover. Two similar looking books, stacked one on top of the other rested on the table next to her mobile phone, cup of coffee and a yellow hi-lighter pen.

After we had finished our drinks and the very tasty breakfast rolls, we left the café, turned left and continued walking along Pentonville Road and came to a crossroads with Caledonian Road on the left and King's Cross Bridge on the right which had the imposing baroque styled Scala nightclub on the corner.

"What's the name of the place we're looking for again, Hugo?"

"The Travelodge Royal Scot at 100 King's Cross Road," replied Hugo, consulting his notebook.

On we trod, and we were both delighted when the next turn on the right was King's Cross Road. We were about to cross over Pentonville Road when we heard the sound of

59

sirens as an ambulance with 'blues and twos' flashing and wailing, raced along at speed to some unseen emergency making us step back. We waited for two red buses; the 205 to Bow Church and then the 63 to Honor Oak and a few cars to pass, before we were able to cross over and walk down King's Cross Road which diverged away from Pentonville Road at a 45-degree angle, the wedge-shaped space left between the two roads being filled by the Honest Burgers restaurant.

After a few more minutes walking, we passed Leeke Street on the right and then I caught sight of the corner of the red brick hotel showing the Travelodge logo and name.

Directly opposite the hotel was an AM2PM Mini Food and Wine shop.

"I'm just gonna pop across to the shop to buy a pint of milk," I hollered to Hugo. I didn't like the milk they have in hotels in those little plastic pots, as they made the tea and coffee taste funny. "Do you want anything?"

"I don't think so, Bert."

Hugo went to the hotel reception to book us in while I crossed over the road by the zebra crossing to buy the milk, which, as usual was located at the back of the shop. Milk bought, I re-crossed the road and entered the hotel through the glass automatic doors to find Hugo still waiting in the queue at reception. So, I went to the bar opposite which also doubled as a dining room, and bought us a pint of Boddingtons Bitter each, and sat down at one of the square wooden topped tables with the white plastic chairs and metal legs. The right-hand side was completely glazed, which afforded a view of a row of shops, and in the far right-hand corner was a wall mounted TV showing one of the news channels with the volume lowered.

Hugo joined me after a while, and after he had sat down and taken a gulp of his beer, he gave me my room key card. I was in room 116 and Hugo was next door in 118 on the first floor.

"Did they ask for our passports?"

"No, Bert, should they have done?"

"Not really, but I've been to various hotels in London and Birmingham from Leicester where I've been asked for my passport. When I queried why I would need my passport when travelling between two cities in England, they told me it was to do with money laundering!"

"The mind boggles, Bert!"

After we had finished our drinks we made our way to our rooms. There was a security door that led to the accommodation area that I had to put the key card in to open. Inside there was a lift but as we were only on the first floor, we walked up the flight of stairs. "I'll see you in the bar at six o'clock, Bert."

"Okay, Hugo," I said, putting my card into the slot to open my room door.

Chapter Eleven

The room was big and bright and had a king-sized bed with four plump pillows, and one of those nondescript riot of colour 'hotel' pictures above it, TV, tea and coffee making facilities, a desk and a white plastic chair with metal legs, the same as the ones in the restaurant. The windows had grey, red and blue striped curtains, and the view overlooked a car park. I dumped my holdall on the bed and took my wash kit out to put in the bathroom which was very white and basic with no toiletries. *Good job I'd brought my own*, I thought.

I made myself a cup of tea and after drinking it I then decided to have a 'power nap', but despite feeling tired I just could not sleep and found myself thinking about Julia for the second time since Friday at the café, and I was hoping I would see her again next week. I got up and made myself another cup of tea and sat at the desk to read my *2000AD* comic. My favourite character was Rogue Trooper, lone survivor of the massacre of the genetic infantrymen, who was hunting the traitorous general who had sold them out. As I was reading, I kept on nodding off, and I decided to try and get some sleep again.

I must have dropped off, as I woke up with a start. Fumbling around on the bedside table, I located my mobile phone to tell the time, I had three watches at home, but I never wore any of them. It was 17:07, time to get up and have a shit, shower and shave, in that order, before meeting Hugo at the bar. It was almost 18:00 by the time I left my room and I was in the bar exactly two minutes later to find Hugo had got the drinks in and was sitting at a table perusing the food menu. The bar-cum-dining room was full of what looked like students and from their conversation I would say they were German from the odd word I recognised.

"Do you know any German Hugo?"

"*Zwei bier bitte.*"

"Hmm very useful, anything else?"

"*Stoppem floppem.*"

"What on earth does that mean?"

"It's German for bra!" Both Hugo and I fell about laughing.

"Cheers, Hugo," I said, as I lifted the pint to my mouth and took a large gulp.

"Cheers, Bert," Hugo replied, doing the same. "I fancy the burger and chips." Hugo then handed me the menu and I looked down the list of meals available, each one appealing to me. "I think I'll have the burger and chips as well." Hugo got up and walked over to the bar to order the food, two more pints and a packet of cheese and onion crisps. "Thanks Hugo," I said as he threw the bag across the table. I opened the bag and proffered it to Hugo.

"No thanks, Bert."

"You know what that means, don't you?"

"No, what?"

"More for me," I said with a smile while picking out a handful and munching on them. "I remember when I was in the Falklands, the only crisps available were called Jakes Pub Crisps but they weren't a patch on Walkers. Anyway, one afternoon a guy newly arrived from England landed with an unopened bag of Walkers Prawn Cocktail crisps and he agreed to auction them. After furious bidding, they were eventually sold for five pounds, and that was in 1993!"

"Two burger and chips?" the waitress enquired as she approached us holding two plates. She was dressed in a turquoise short-sleeved blouse, which was open at the neck, and dark-blue trousers.

"Yes, that's us," Hugo replied, raising his hand. The waitress set down the plates and cutlery on the table.

"Can I get you anything else?"

"No, that's everything, thank you," Hugo replied.

"Enjoy your meal," she said with a smile as she walked back the way she came.

The condiments were housed in a black plastic container with, 'It has to be Heinz' printed on it and was full of sachets of vinegar, mayonnaise and tomato ketchup, but no brown sauce or mustard. I took two sachets of mayonnaise and squirted it over my chips. Hugo and I both tucked into our meal with gusto and washed it down with another pint from the bar.

"Do you fancy a walk out to find a pub, Bert?"

"Yes, I could do with stretching my legs," I said wiping my mouth on the napkin that came wrapped around the knife and fork, as Hugo drained the last of his pint and then we were ready to explore. As Hugo got up from the table he bent down and picked up his rucksack from underneath it and hefted it onto his shoulder. "What *are* you bringing that for?" I said with a sigh.

"Well, I don't wanna leave *it* in the hotel, do I Bert?"

"Whatever," I said with another sigh and shake of my head.

Chapter Twelve

The sun was still strong and bright in the cloudless blue sky as we left the hotel. A waxing silvery moon was about seventy-five per cent visible and looked as if someone had purposefully placed it there so the vast expanse of the sky wouldn't look so empty. Gazing up at the moon reminded me of the time a boyhood friend of mine told me his parents had given him everything that he had asked for – money, clothes, toys, etc., until the day he had asked for the moon!

We walked over the zebra crossing and turning right leisurely strolled up King's Cross Road past the Northumberland Arms pub and then, at the top turned left into Pentonville Road.

"I saw some pubs on Caledonian Road," said Hugo.

"Okay, we'll check them out," I answered as we turned right into Caledonian Road. Next to the Keystone House Hostel on the corner was a black painted pub called The Scottish Stores. Outside was a sandwich board, advertising a rooftop terrace that was open until 10 pm. We went inside, and it looked quite small and narrow but inviting with its wood panelling and wide range of craft beers, but I didn't like the thought of sitting on the uncomfortable looking stools as they always left me with a bad back.

"Let's try somewhere else, Hugo, I can't be doing with stools," I said as we left.

"Okay, Bert, I don't like sitting on stools myself. There's another pub a bit further up on the other side." I looked up the road and saw it had wooden picnic-like tables with attached benches outside for *al fresco* drinking.

Millers was a sports bar on the corner of Caledonian Road and Caledonia Street. Hugo immediately went inside while I sat down at one of the tables underneath the dark blue Heineken awning, which gave some relief from the heat and faced away from the Tesco Metro store on the opposite side of Caledonia Street. After a good ten minutes Hugo joined me and set two froth-topped pints of beer down on the table. "What kept you?" I enquired.

"It's quite busy in there actually, I hope you like John Smiths, Bert?"

"Yes, that's fine, Hugo. What's it like inside?"

"Not bad actually, Bert, a bit noisy and a bit on the dark side, but down to earth with say a fifty-fifty mix of both locals and tourists, and it has three plasma TVs showing Sky Sports."

"Sounds a bit lively then. It's quite nice sitting out here in the shade enjoying a relaxing pint, better than being cooped up in the hotel," I replied.

"Yes, it's lovely, Bert."

"Who was playing?"

"Oh, I didn't take much notice, I was too busy trying to get served."

"You know how much I like the Human League, Bert?"

"Yes, I do, Hugo," I replied. "I quite like them as well."

"Well, I saw them on an edition of *Top of the Pops* from 1983 the other day singing 'Keep Feeling Fascination', and Phil Oakey had more make-up on than the two female singers put together!"

"I saw that episode and noticed the amount of make-up he wore, and felt the same." Hugo just shook his head as he took a long gulp of his pint and wiped the froth from his mouth.

"You do know that we have a standing invitation to visit Blodwyn in Wales, don't you, Hugo?" Blodwyn Pugh was an old RAF buddy of mine and was always asking me when Hugo and I were going to visit her.

"Yes, we shall have to arrange to go and see her," Hugo said, nodding his head. "And visit the *Doctor Who* Experience, Bert?"

"You'll have no problems there, as she's a big *Doctor Who* fan herself."

"Great!" said Hugo, executing a 'fist pump'. "Where about in Wales does she live?"

"In a village called North Cornelly, which is near Bridgend. From Leicester by train you have to change at Birmingham and Cardiff and get off at a place called Pyle, which is the nearest train station. The whole journey takes just under four and a half hours."

"Have you considered going by National Express?"

"I hadn't really thought about that option, but it's something to consider, I suppose, Hugo."

"Is it anywhere near Portmeirion, Bert?"

"Nowhere near, I'm afraid, Number Six," I joshed.

"That's a place I should like to visit someday, Bert."

"And me," I replied.

As the sun began to slowly go down and the light started to lose its colour, we decided to move inside the pub. "What are you having, Hugo?" Hugo looked at the beer names displayed on the name tags attached to the pump handles; as well as John Smith's there was Coast to Coast, Blue Moon and London Pride to choose from.

"I'll try the Blue Moon, Bert," he said after much deliberation.

"Two pints of Blue Moon, please," I said to the bearded barman dressed all in black. He poured the drinks and placed the two tall Blue Moon logoed glasses on the counter. "That'll be £8, please." I paid him and sat down next to Hugo.

"Cheers, Bert."

"Cheers, Hugo," I said as we both took a sip.

"What's this?" Hugo said, picking something out of his glass. I looked inside mine and noticed it was a half slice of orange. Hugo dropped his back in the glass when he recognised what it was, and resumed drinking.

"That's a nice pint, Bert."

"Yes, it tastes lovely, good choice, Hugo," I replied, savouring the taste. The interior of the pub was exactly how Hugo had described it and also featured a two-step wooden platform surrounded by a wooden balustrade in front of the windows, which faced Caledonian Road and housed three tables, all occupied by couples. Along the bar, men sat on stools chatting or turned around to watch the TV screens, which on one was the quarter-final France versus Iceland football match, of the Euro 2016 tournament. The other screens showed pundits in a studio discussing other matches. The rest of the customers just sat at the tables chatting and drinking their pints or bottled beers.

"Have you ever seen those films or documentaries where scuba divers sit on the edge of a boat and then fall backwards into the sea?"

"And here, below the tropical waters of the Indian Ocean, we see the Tuna fish in its natural habitat, but predators are never far away," Hugo said, mimicking Sir David Attenborough. "Yes, I have actually, Bert."

"Do you know *why* they fall in backwards, Hugo?"

"I never gave it much thought."

"It's because if they fall forwards they would land in the bottom of the boat!"

"Har de har, Bert, very funny," said Hugo, sounding unamused, but his mouth betrayed him with the faint trace of a smile. "I thought you were gonna tell me something educational or scientific then."

"Yeah, right," I replied with a laugh.

We stayed in the bar for the rest of the evening drinking Blue Moon and when Hugo announced it was ten to eleven, we drank up and left as we had a big day ahead of us tomorrow.

Chapter Thirteen

It was dark when we left the pub, the graphite coloured sky was starless with patchy clouds and the moon suspended there as before. As we crossed to the other side of the road, two men appeared out of a bus shelter next to a pizza restaurant and stood in front of us, blocking our way.

The first was tall and gaunt looking with hollow cheeks, and had a face like an angry weasel, with grey hair tied in a ponytail, a grey moustache and a straggly beard and looked a lot older than he probably was. He wore a black distressed looking leather jacket with an elasticated waistband and zippered sleeves, which was way too big for him over a grey hoody, and a pair of baggy darker grey tracksuit bottoms tucked into black socks with dirty white trainers. He held a roll-up between his nicotine-stained fingers.

The second man was shorter and more heavily built and had dreadlocks tucked up into a blue peaked Rasta hat with a black, red, yellow and green band around the middle and wore a pull-over hoody in the same colours, striped vertically on the body and horizontally on the arms, and a pair of ex-army DPM combat trousers, which fell over scuffed black boots with untied laces. Slung across his back by the cord was a red CEX bag.

"Have you got a spare cigarette, man?" Weasel asked.

"No, I don't smoke and neither does my friend," I answered.

"What's in the rucksack?"

"Just dirty washing, we were looking for a late-night launderette," Hugo replied.

"Looks like we've got ourselves a pair of wise guys," Weasel hissed to Dreadlocks with a cheerless grin. Dreadlocks grunted, as his eyes darted around for any signs of interference in their business. "Hand over the rucksack, man!" Weasel demanded.

"Suck my Richard!" Hugo retorted. Weasel's grin rapidly faded.

"Hand over the rucksack man!" he repeated with more than a hint of menace and, taking a long drag on his cigarette, he puffed out the blue tinged smoke directly into Hugo's face. I thought Hugo was going to head butt him, but he calmly stood his ground like 'Stonewall' Jackson at the First Battle of Bull Run. Hugo looked at me and gave me a wink and then slowly unhooked the strap of the rucksack off his right shoulder and held it out tantalisingly in front of him. Weasel took a step closer and held out his hand to take the rucksack from Hugo's extended hand and on the point of handing it over, Hugo dropped it.

"Oops!" said Hugo as the rucksack landed with a soft thud on the pavement.

"You shouldn't have done that man, now pick it up!"

"You want it, you pick it up!" Hugo balled his hands into fists, his knuckles turning white.

"Now I'll ask you for the last time, man, pick up the rucksack!" Weasel snarled, exposing what rotten teeth he had left. To back up his demand he produced a cruel looking knife from his pocket, the long metal blade gleaming menacingly in the light cast from a nearby lamp post.

Suddenly, from my right, it appeared as if the darkness had come alive as a black clad figure sprang out of nowhere, disturbing the warm night air as he passed me and

71

positioned himself between Hugo and the knife-wielding Weasel. "Bloody hell…it's Darth Vader!" Hugo cried.

Quick as a flash, the newcomer grabbed hold of Weasel's spindly wrist, which held the knife, and squeezed it tightly until he yelped in pain and the knife fell from his hand and clattered onto the pavement. He then followed it up with an open palm thrust, the power of which came straight from his powerful shoulder and smashed it into Weasel's nose like a brick through glass, breaking it with a teeth-jarring, sickening crack and spraying crimson coloured blood high into the air. This sent him tottering backwards and after a few more steps he collapsed in a heap onto the pavement. "You've broken my nose, man!" Weasel screamed through the pain, cupping his hands over his shattered nose, the blood ran down his chin like ketchup from a hotdog and stained the front of his hoody a slick violent crimson.

Seeing that Weasel had been injured and enraged that his comrade-in-crime had failed to secure the rucksack, Dreadlocks launched himself at Weasel's assailant but was stopped instantly in his tracks when a well-timed, highly polished boot swiftly connected with his groin. His face contorted in agony as his legs buckled underneath him, and with tears streaming from his eyes, he dropped heavily to his knees and then slowly rolled over onto his right side like a capsizing ship. Dreadlocks writhed about on the pavement clutching his genitals, desperately trying to soothe the pain that burned deep inside them and howling like a wounded animal.

It had been a brief one-sided fight and Hugo and I looked on as the two wannabe muggers slowly got to their feet and staggered off to lick their wounds. Supporting each other, they quickly disappeared into the darkness, muttering garbled curses, with Weasel leaving a dot-to-dot trail of blood spatters along the pavement.

Chapter Fourteen

The black clad figure was at the least 6' 2" tall, muscular and was dressed in SWAT style, black clothing and equipment. I thought he looked more like Karl Urban's portrayal of Judge Dredd, rather than Darth Vader with his tactical military helmet, tinted safety goggles worn over a hood, which left only that portion of his face from his philtrum to his chin exposed. He was clean shaven and square jawed, and wore 'hard knuckle' gloves, with elbow and knee protector pads. A tactical vest with numerous pockets, which were no doubt full of crime fighting gadgets and gizmos, was worn over a zip-fronted boiler suit, with the bottom of the legs 'bloused' over high-leg Magnum boots, and to top it all he also wore …a cape!"

"Thank you for your help back there, do you have a name…friend?" Hugo said.

'Justice Never Sleeps,' he said standing with his legs apart and his hands on his hips with his head held high, his voice sounding like he'd eaten a bowl of gravel for breakfast, but more likely he'd had three shredded wheat.

"Doesn't exactly roll off the tongue, Justice Never Sleeps, does it?" I said.

"What you need is something a bit more…punchier," Hugo chipped in. "Something like…Urban Justice or even Street Justice." "Crime never sleeps, so justice *must* never sleep," Justice replied.

"Isn't the cape a bit…theatrical?" said Hugo. I cringed as Justice shot Hugo a look.

"This is my 'Black Cape of Justice'," he declared, then grabbed it by the edge and pulled it across his body like it had magical powers or was bullet proof or something, and then posed like he was modelling for the front cover of a comic book. There was a short pregnant pause and then all three of us burst into laughter.

Hugo picked up his rucksack and brushed it down.

"If they wanted a few towels that badly, all they had to do was ask nicely." He then unzipped his rucksack and pulled out what looked like the white towels from the hotel.

"You might have told me you weren't carrying the idol, Hugo! For one mad moment there I thought you were about to hand it over."

"Do you think I'm crazy enough to walk around the streets of London with a solid gold statuette in my rucksack, Bert?" I desperately wanted to say yes.

"No, of course not, Hugo," I lied.

"Do you think they were just a pair of no marks trying their luck on finding something valuable to sell for booze or drugs, or was the encounter deliberately engineered because they somehow knew *what* we were carrying, Bert?"

"Hard to tell at present," I replied.

Justice picked up the unbloodied knife from the pavement that Weasel had dropped, studied it and then dropped it down the nearest drain cover.

"Listen," Hugo said to Justice "we could do with your help if you're available to watch our backs when we deliver our package tomorrow."

"Give me the when and where and I'll see what I can do, but I'm making no promises."

"That's fine by me," Hugo said, passing him the details of our rendezvous with the Fatman.

"Thanks again, Justice, for all you're…" Hugo stopped abruptly when he realised he was talking to himself. Justice had disappeared as quickly into the darkness as he had appeared out of it. "I was just going to say thanks once again. What did you make of our friend, Bert?"

"Yeah, he seems like a good guy to have on your side, but it's probably not sugar he sprinkles on his cereal. I think you have to be a bit crazy, anyway, to do what he does."

"Why do you think he does do it Bert, knowing that one night he might be seriously injured, or even...killed?"

"Hmm, that's a tricky one Hugo. Maybe he, a friend or a family member has been the victim of crime and the criminals have gone unpunished by the law; he might get a hard on from dressing up; he has a genuine passion for patrolling the streets, keeping them safe, or maybe he just simply gets a buzz from kicking the crap out of wrongdoers, who knows? The reasons are endless."

"Ain't that the truth?" Hugo said, as we started to walk along Pentonville Road and then on into King's Cross Road to return to our hotel.

"So where *is* the idol, Hugo?"

"It's back at the hotel, but it's well hidden in a place nobody would dream of looking in," said Hugo, as we arrived at the hotel without further incident.

"I think we deserve a night cap, Bert."

"Yes Hugo, I think we do." Hugo went straight to the bar and ordered two double Southern Comforts with ice.

"Cheers, Bert."

"Cheers, Hugo." We clinked our glasses together and as I took a sip of the smooth gold coloured liquid, an instant warming feeling spread inside of me.

"So, shall we see if the idol is still in its *secret* place Hugo?"

"I was just about to check, Bert; do you think we might have had some visitors then?"

"Stands a good chance."

We left the bar and walked up the stairs and along the corridor to Hugo's room, where he inserted his key card into the slot of the door, opened it gingerly and turned on the light. He went straight into the bathroom and removed the cover of the toilet cistern and lifted out a Tesco plastic carrier bag from the water. Taking out a towel from his rucksack, Hugo wiped the bag dry, threw the towel on the side of the bath, and then to my utter amazement pulled out the dry golden idol. "I shall sleep with it next to me tonight, Bert."

"Whatever floats your boat, Hugo. Has anything been moved that you know of?" Hugo looked around the room. "No, everything looks the same as I left it."

"Okay, I'll see you in the morning."

"Goodnight John Boy." Hugo called out as I left his room.

"Goodnight Jim Bob," I replied with a smile. I hadn't the heart to tell Hugo that any thief worth his salt, after searching his room and finding nothing, wouldn't have left without checking the cistern.

Chapter Fifteen

I was woken up by the sound of the alarm from my mobile phone. I reached over to turn it off; it was 07:00, time to get up. I took a sip of water from the glass I had put on the bedside table last night, together with some paracetamol, but my head was fine, and I lay back down in bed. It had been a warm night even with the window open, and so I had stripped the bed of the bedding, bar one sheet. The air conditioning wasn't an option because of the racket it made, so I had turned it off. I couldn't even bear the sound of a ticking clock at night, and don't get me started about ex-partners who snored like drunken sailors.

After ten more minutes in bed I got up and showered, shaved, added a splash of David Beckham aftershave, and got dressed. There was a knock at the door just as I was packing the last of my gear into my holdall. I glanced around the room one last time to check I had everything and then opened the door.

"Morning, Bert, ready for the day ahead?" Hugo said, beaming. I disliked cheerful people first thing in the morning. Hugo was more soberly dressed in a US style chocolate-brown coloured leather flying jacket with knitted cuffs and waistband and two large side pockets with stud fastenings, plus two slash 'hand warmer' pockets worn over a plain pale-blue shirt with black trousers and his three buckle boots.

"Morning, Hugo. Yeah, I am thanks…you?"

"Yes, Bert, I slept like a log."

"Have you got the idol?"

"Yes, it's back in my rucksack. Let's go and get some breakfast, Bert, I'm starving!"

I closed the door and we walked down the stairs to the breakfast room, which was swarming with the German students we had seen last night while having a drink in the hotel bar. We made our way to the self-service area, but there wasn't much left of anything. The words 'plague' and 'locusts' danced across my retinas as I surveyed the scene. There were only some beans and a few rashers of bacon left, which we put on our plates. There were no fruit juices, just the empty jugs, and from the number of cups stacked up around the coffee machine it looked like there was no coffee either. I looked around for a member of staff but couldn't find anyone. Hugo and I found a table with the least amount of mess on it.

"I was really looking forward to breakfast," I said.

"Me too, Bert, never mind, we'll stop and have something to eat before we meet the Fatman."

After we ate our meagre breakfast, which didn't take long, Hugo checked us out and we then left the hotel, stepping out into the glorious shimmering sunshine with high flying airliners criss-crossing noiselessly through the cloudless blue sky, leaving long multi vapour trails in their wake on their way to distant shores.

"Keep your eyes peeled, for our friend from the train."

"Will do, Bert," said Hugo stopping to put his designer sunglasses on, as we started to make our way back up King's Cross Road.

It seemed the whole of London was going to work, with the majority probably like us heading for the tube station at King's Cross. The first thing I noticed was that most people were carrying a cup of coffee in a waxed paper cup in one hand and their mobile phone in the other, either talking or furiously texting away with their head down, not looking where they were going. It always amazed me how they could hold their phone in one hand and, using the thumb of the same hand, type at lightning fast speed. It took me all my time to hold the phone in one hand and type with the other and that could only be accomplished by standing still! Others just walked along doing nothing or listening to music, using ear pieces or headphones.

I was quite surprised at the number of women who were elegantly dressed in smart jackets and skirts or trouser-suits trekking to work with a rucksack on their back and wearing brightly coloured trainers! At work they would then exchange the trainers for their killer heels.

We walked along King's Cross Road and then turned left onto Pentonville Road, passing Caledonian Road where we had the 'scuffle' last night. We reached King's Cross St. Pancras underground station and went down the steps to the underground itself, where we had to queue at the ticket machines for a while before it was our turn. Hugo tapped in 'Lambeth North' in the destination block on the touch screen and then 'single' and then 'confirm'. The screen showed £4.90 and Hugo fed in a fiver and a pink card ticket and a 10p coin fell into the well. Hugo retrieved them and gave me the ticket and repeated the process for himself.

"What's the best way to get to Lambeth North?" asked Hugo, to the underground staff member with the Mohican hair style.

"Take the Northern Line to the Elephant & Castle and then change for the Bakerloo Line."

"Thanks," Hugo replied. We fed our tickets into the ticket barrier and followed the signs for the Northern Line. We went down the escalator, turned right and right again, following the white tiled winding corridors and, after going down another escalator, we came to a junction for the northbound and southbound platforms. After reading the list of stations, the Elephant & Castle station was seven stops away, and we needed to turn right for the southbound platform 8.

We arrived on the platform and became part of the crowd waiting to board the next train, well, more like hoping to board the next train. There must have been hundreds of people spread along the entire length of the platform. I had been on the underground trains in Tokyo, but this was much worse.

The trains that arrived were absolutely packed solid; sardines had more room than the hapless commuters crammed into the carriages. We sat down on some grey metal seats and let three packed trains go by before we felt confident that we were able to board the next one, and even then, it was like trying to squeeze a quart into a pint pot. I held on for my life as the automatic doors shut and the train pulled out of the station with a jolt. Over the tannoy, a female voice announced, "This is a Northern Line train terminating at Morden."

The carriage rocked from side-to-side, as the train trundled along through the dark labyrinths of the underground system. The interior was stifling and what little air there was circulating, was very pungent with the smells of sweat, coffee, the sickly, sweet aroma of energy drinks and an assortment of aftershaves and perfumes as passengers moved around and against each other to get on or off at the stations. I, myself, was having to constantly wipe the sweat from my forehead with some napkins from the hotel restaurant.

Despite the lack of room, some of the passengers somehow managed to drink, read their kindles and newspapers or listen to music on their headphones and earpieces, while the majority just stood there looking vacuous and probably thinking that Monday morning had come around again all too quickly. I stood there holding onto a handrail watching them, thinking that this is what they must go through to get to work and the same again to get back home, Monday to Friday.

The train stopped at Angel, Old Street and Moorgate stations, where it seemed more people got on than got off, and then suddenly at Bank station a whole load of people got off, and to our relief we were able to find some seats next to a man tapping away on his laptop, which was perched on his knees, and finally sit down.

"I couldn't put up with this each day, Bert."

"I was just thinking the same, and that's before you even start work. They must be accustomed to it."

"I wonder what it's like by bus?"

"I shudder to think, Hugo."

Two more stops followed at London Bridge and Borough before the female voice announced, "The next station is Elephant and Castle, change here for Bakerloo Line and national rail services." We got off and then followed the signs for the Bakerloo Line and the northbound platform 4 to take us to the next stop and the end of our journey, which was Lambeth North. At the station we alighted and followed the 'Way Out' signs that led up the stairs and along the corridor and into the waiting lift, where there were already a lot of people waiting inside. We were the last ones to enter and the doors closed behind us. After a few seconds the doors in front of us opened and we all walked out and had to queue for a bit to go through the sole 'out' ticket barrier one after the other, and we were forced to listen to a raven-haired woman talking in detail to a blonde that JFK was her historical crush.

Chapter Sixteen

Once outside the station, Hugo discreetly pointed across Kennington Road to the shop where the drop off was to take place but, as we were early we turned right as there was a Costa on the other side of the road below the tall and boxy shaped Tune Hotel. I pressed the button on the pedestrian crossing at what looked like a star-shaped major road intersection. The top point sweeping down to the lower right point was Westminster Bridge Road; immediately to our front was the upper right point of Baylis Road which continued through to the upper left point and became Hercules Road, and the lower left point was Kennington Road.

We both stood there feeling like spectators at the Tour de France, waiting for the 'man' to turn green. A great sweating mass of lycra covered cyclists swept past us at break-neck speed. Dressed mostly in luminous tight-fitting lime, lemon or orange coloured Hi-Viz jerseys and an assortment of different coloured tight lycra leggings in thigh, calf and ankle length versions and fingerless mitts topped off with streamlined 'go faster' helmets in various shades and patterns, they made a colourful sight racing to work on drop handled cycles where they could shower and then change into their business suits before starting work. It always made me smile that they wore all this Hi-Viz clothing and then wore a dark coloured rucksack on their back.

Following on close behind were those cyclists who liked to travel at a more leisurely pace than the 'lycra brigade' and weren't so sportily dressed or fashion conscious. Yes, the majority wore Hi-Viz clothing but not as garish or tight, with some showing exposed skin between their tops and bottoms, and quite a few exhibited a visible pantie line while others just wore a simple Hi-Viz vest with silver reflective strips that you could buy from any of the various 'pound' shops along with a variety of colourful helmets. The cycles in the main seemed less sporty as well, with straight handle bars plus baskets and panniers either on the front, rear or sides, together with a smattering of the silver and blue unisex cycles of the public hire scheme called Santander Cycles, which were more popularly known as 'Boris bikes' after Boris Johnson, the former Mayor of London.

When the 'man' eventually flashed green, we crossed Baylis Road and, as it was warm, I sat outside on the silver metal chairs with matching circular tables under the maroon-coloured awning while Hugo disappeared inside to buy the coffees. I immediately removed the glass ash tray to another table, I didn't mind people smoking, I just disliked ash trays.

On the opposite side of the road that we had just crossed, below the constantly changing billboard, there was a green LCD display showing the time, which was 09:10 alternatively with the temperature, which read 18°C and was very comfortable. Further along to the left were some maroon painted forty-five gallon drums, some whole and some cut in half, with flowers and shrubs planted in them which I thought was a novel way of putting to good use otherwise scrap oil drums. Next to them was a docking station for a row of 'Boris' bikes.

A grey haired, impatient old man wearing a beige, belted mackintosh despite the warm weather, was shuffling across the pedestrian crossing after the lights had changed to red and had almost made it to the pavement nearest the Costa, when a cyclist came round the corner at high speed, he shouted a warning to the old man, but it was too late and he clipped the side of him, hit the curb and was sent flying over the handle bars as though he had been shot out of a circus cannon, and hit the pavement with a 'thwack', rolled over and was back on his feet before I had time to get out of my seat to assist him.

"Are you all right, chap?" I enquired.

"Yes, I'm good, thanks," he said, rubbing his right elbow. He wore a chromed helmet and was brightly dressed in lycra with, oddly a pair of black conventional shorts worn over his leggings, which I was certain he wore to cover up his manhood.

"Is your bike okay?" the old man said in a wheezy voice, who appeared uninjured and seemed more concerned for the machine rather than the man. The cyclist gave his bike the once over, paying particular attention to the wheels.

"Yes, it's fine, are you all right?"

"So, your bike's okay, then?" the old man repeated.

"Yes," the cyclist said again, and, with that, the old man shuffled off without another word. The cyclist looked at me and gave a shrug as if it were par for the course of cycling in London, and then mounted his cycle and with a wave rode off. I'd seen a lot of instances on my many visits to London where impatient pedestrians were stepping out into the road whenever and wherever they pleased, whether at a pedestrian crossing showing red or frantically dodging between buses, cars and cyclists alike, not only putting themselves in danger, but other road users.

Hugo then appeared with a tray of coffees, toasties and crisps and set them down on the table, totally unaware of what had happened in his absence.

"The other night, I went to a wine bar and got chatting to a woman who told me she was a barrister. The next morning, I popped into my local Costa for a coffee and there was the woman serving behind the counter. I said to her 'I thought you told me you were a barrister', to which she replied, 'No, I said I was a barista!' Although I'd heard the joke before I still laughed, as did Hugo."

"There's a barista who works at one of the Costa's back home who doesn't even like coffee. Every time a customer asks her a question about a certain type of coffee, she has to ask another member of staff, who then has to explain it to the customer."

"That's gotta be wrong, Bert. I got us some toasties as I don't know when we will have a chance to eat again."

"Thanks, Hugo, what are they?" I said taking a bite out of the toasted snack.

"Cumberland sausage and caramelised red onion."

"Mmm, they're very nice."

"Yes, they are rather moreish, Bert," Hugo said while chewing noisily.

"You missed all the action while you were being served," I said, opening the bag of Tyrrells mature cheddar and chive crisps.

"What action, Bert?"

"An old guy and a cyclist had a collision right in front of me. I thought the cyclist was joining me for coffee the way he flew off his bike and just missed the chair."

"Was anyone injured?"

"The old guy didn't appear to be hurt and was more interested in the condition of the cycle than its rider, and the cyclist said he was good, but was nursing his elbow."

"Good job it was a bike and not a bus! They're both lucky it wasn't more serious, Bert."

"Too right, I hate the sight of blood. These crisps are nice," I said, munching on them between mouthfuls of toastie.

"I should think so, Bert, for £1 a bag!"

"Blimey! I'm just gonna quickly nip to the loo, Hugo," I said rising from my seat.

"Hurry up, then, as it's a quarter to ten now," Hugo said impatiently, looking at his watch. "Time, we made a move, Bert."

"I'll only be a minute," I answered.

I quickly re-joined Hugo outside the Costa as the 'man' glowed green, and we re-crossed carefully over the busy Baylis Road at the pedestrian crossing that the old man had so nearly been mown down on. We then crossed Westminster Bridge Road, curving around the grey, gothic looking Lincoln Tower and then crossed Kennington Road. Walking along the right-hand side, we passed a long row of shops.

"Here we are," Hugo said, coming to a halt. The shop was sandwiched between a betting shop and a barbers and was almost directly opposite Kennington Police Station and, as if to reinforce the point, a police Ford Transit van was parked outside.

"KC (International) Foods Limited," said Hugo, reading the sign.

"Quality Foods and Spices from around the World," I added, reading the next line. The lettering had been removed but had left a black outline against the peeling and grimy, once white paint and so was readable. The shop looked as if it had been closed for a long time. A battered wood and sun-faded blue canvas awning was folded back above the sign. The large windows on either side of the red door had been boarded up. Above the door was what looked like vintage metal advertising signs, probably from the sixties or early seventies for Brooke Bond Tea and Crown Cup Coffee.

"Ready, Hugo?"

"I'm a bit nervous, but I'll be okay," he answered as he pressed the button on the new looking intercom. I must admit I was feeling a bit anxious myself but didn't let it show.

"Hello?" said a female voice.

"Hugo Twiss, I've got an appointment with the Fatman."

"Push the door," the voice instructed. There was a buzzing noise as the door was released from its magnetic catch, and Hugo pushed the door open and we both stepped inside the former shop.

Chapter Seventeen

The inside had been emptied of all the shop furniture and was cool but smelt of air freshener. Two floor-to-ceiling metal stanchions stood like forlorn sentinels in the middle of the room. There were no other windows and the lighting was provided by unshaded fluorescent tubes which bathed the room in an unnatural harsh, yellow luminosity, while a shaft of natural daylight came from a skylight.

Along the far wall was a red door that probably led to an office-cum-storage area, together with some toilets, and along the right-hand wall stood what looked like two wooden wall papering tables and a number of metal stacking chairs. One of the tables displayed a selection of cereal bars, fruit, yoghurt, bottled orange juice and water, together with tea and coffee making facilities and paper plates, Styrofoam cups, plastic cutlery and paper napkins, and the other was covered with a cheap white tablecloth, on which sat a desktop fan that moved from side-to-side, humming noisily.

Helping themselves to the refreshments were a man and a woman which left me feeling a bit puzzled. The woman was, I reckoned in her thirties, attractive and curvy, medium height, and had short blonde hair which was turning brassy. Her full lips sported pink lipstick, and she was wearing a washed out blue denim jacket over a pink top with tight fitting blue jeans that, though I could never figure out why, were fashionably ripped at the knees. A pair of flat red shoes and a large red bag dangling by the handles over her left shoulder completed her outfit.

The man was mixed race with short black hair and made determining his age easy by having '1981' tattooed on the back of his neck, he also displayed a tattoo of a small winged parachute on his right forearm which was the cap badge of the Parachute Regiment. He was tall with broad shoulders and looked like he still kept himself physically fit and had *the* look of being ex-forces. He also had tribal pattern tattoos on his muscular upper arms, and around his right wrist he had a 'Help for Heroes' wristband, as did Hugo and I, and was wearing a black polo necked shirt and black trousers with large cargo pockets and black shoes. A plain black holdall squatted between his feet.

"We've been expecting you, Mr Twiss and Mr err…" A man I assumed was the mysterious 'Fatman' said amiably.

"Shannon, Rick Shannon," I cut in.

"My name is Desmond Gladwyn Anderson, but better known to one and all as the Fatman."

"Mis-ter An-der-son…I've always wanted to say that," Hugo said stretching out the syllables of his name as he strode forward holding out his hand to shake the Fatman's hand, but the gesture was ignored, and he sat there wiping his brow. "Bit of an understatement wasn't it, Hugo?" I whispered.

"What was?"

"Calling him the Fatman, *he's* even bigger than Tubbs Tubbson, the man who played a planet and *he's* got more chins than China!" Hugo had to struggle hard to stifle himself from laughing out loud. The Fatman was squeezed into the seat of a top of the range three-wheeled mobility scooter in black with silver trim, wing mirrors and a single headlight that from the front made it look like a motor bike.

The Fatman looked about sixty, was tanned with a large fleshy face that housed small beady eyes, and was bald on top, with long greasy hair at the back and sides, which fell like a curtain over his ears and shoulders; his forehead seemed to be permanently beaded with perspiration. He looked as if he had no neck as his head seemed to morph into his shoulders, and had large meaty hands with fingers like sausages. He wore a brilliant white track suit with three parallel blue lines running down the outside of the sleeves and legs and black booty-type slippers with Velcro fasteners. In his mouth he had one of those e-pipes which looked just like a traditional tobacco pipe and, when he exhaled, clouds of white smoke came belching out like the *Flying Scotsman* at full speed. "Where's his white cat with the diamond encrusted collar?"

"He's probably in the back, Bert, devouring some Siamese fighting fish for breakfast."

"Or the Fatman's eaten it between two pieces of crusty bread," I countered. Hugo snickered.

"Let me introduce you both to my wife, Dolores," the Fatman said. Dolores Anderson was in her mid-to-late forties I guessed, and looked toned, tanned and also high maintenance. She was very attractive with high cheek bones and bright-blue eyes that sparkled like sapphires and had long shaggy black hair parted in the middle. Her legs were shapely dancer's legs, but it had probably been a long time since she had last danced the hokey cokey with her husband. When she smiled, only the right hand-side of her sensual mouth curled up, which was rather appealing. She wore a wedding ring with a rock the size of a baby's fist and a tight red dress which clung to every curve of her shapely body, which looked as if it had been sprayed on, revealing that she wore no bra; black patent leather high heels completed the picture. Hugo and I shook her soft, elegant hand.

"Nice tan, Dolores, have you been somewhere nice?" I commented.

"Among other places, Cinque Terre."

"Very nice."

"Have you heard of it?"

"Yes, it's a collection of five ancient villages that have colourful houses and vineyards clinging to the steep cliffs in the coastal region of Liguria in north-west Italy. It's also one of the few tourist destinations in the world to have a tourist cap to limit the amount of people visiting the place."

"I'm impressed, Mister Shannon," Dolores replied, looking me up and down and giving me another of her lop-sided smiles.

"Have you been getting cosy with Judith Chalmers?" asked Hugo.

"Lol," I said, smiling. "I saw it on a late-night travel programme on the BBC."

"He must have a big c…." Hugo said out of the corner of his mouth.

"Cheque book?" I cut in before he could finish. "He has a big everything, Hugo!"

"I *was* going to say cheque book, actually, Bert," Hugo said, smirking

"Of course, you were, Hugo."

"Please help yourselves to refreshments, gentlemen," the Fatman interrupted, and drove his scooter which made a whirring noise like a remote-controlled toy car over to the refreshments table. We walked over to the table and I helped myself to a bottle of orange juice and a Kellogg's Nutri-Grain blueberry breakfast bar, while Hugo made himself a coffee.

"Gentlemen, let me introduce you to Miss Parsons," the Fatman interrupted again.

"Please call me Lorraine," the blonde replied in a soft, pleasant voice.

"And this is Mister Holland."

"My friends call me Dutch," he said, holding out his hand. In the armed forces there was a set of nicknames for servicemen with a certain surname. Thus 'Dutch' was applied to anyone with the surname Holland, Whites were called 'Chalky', Smiths were called 'Smudge', Rogers were called 'Buck'; there was a whole list of them. Then there were nicknames which were the opposite of a serviceman's physical attributes, so, if you were tall you were called 'Tiny', fat you were 'Slim', and bald you were 'Curly'. If you didn't fall into those two groups, then there were always the regional nicknames like Taff, Jock, Geordie, Scouse, etc. We all shook hands with each other.

"Now that the introductions are over, we can begin with the business at hand. I believe you all have a package for me?" said the Fatman, gesturing to the empty table with the fan on it.

"I thought there was only one golden idol?" Hugo asked.

"As a security measure, two additional idols, which were just gold-plated and indistinguishable from the original, were produced and as none of you were aware of the existence of the other two, you would protect your idol as if it were solid gold. Don't worry, you will all receive the same fee."

"Did you also have somebody following us?" I said.

"You spotted him – Mister Shannon?"

"We couldn't be one hundred per cent certain, but he had been in the same pub as us on Friday and was on the same train as us leaving Leicester yesterday, then we lost him."

"As another security measure each of you were assigned a 'guardian' to make sure nobody attempted to relieve you of your idol. Your guardian, Mister Twiss, was on hand when you and Mister Shannon were accosted by two ruffians last night and was just about to intervene on your behalf when some black clad vigilante figure got involved, I am told. Did anybody else notice they had someone following them?"

"No," both Dutch and Lorraine answered, looking at each other and shaking their heads.

Chapter Eighteen

Hugo, Dutch and Lorraine placed their bags on the table, removed the idols from them and unwrapped them from their protective coverings. I noticed Hugo's idol was wrapped in the same green towel as before and then all three of the idols were placed carefully on the white cover of the table in front of them. The Fatman's eyes burned with a golden fascination at the sight of the three idols.

"Dolores, my dear, can you please ask Mr Diamond to join us?"

"Of course, Desmond," she replied and turned on her heels and disappeared behind the red door.

"Who's Mister Diamond?" Dutch asked the question before I did.

"Mister Diamond, contrary to his name, is a goldsmith I use from time to time and he's here today to verify that one of the idols, is, in fact, solid gold!" I imagined Mister Diamond, because of his name, was someone in a flash suit with the persona of a game show host, all charm, gleaming teeth and witty one liners.

"And behind the red door tonight…" Hugo quipped as the door opened. Following behind Dolores was a short, timid and rather anonymous looking man with a swarthy complexion and, although it was still morning, was already showing signs of a five o'clock shadow, which by five o'clock would probably be a beard, and had a shock of wavy black hair flecked with grey that made his hair appear as if it was made of wire wool. His eyebrows were black and very bushy, and he wore round, black framed glasses and was dressed in a rather sombre looking brown suit, the only splash of colour being provided by a red bow tie. In his right hand he clutched a brown leather briefcase.

"Ah, Benny, there you are," said the Fatman.

"Nice to see you again, Desmond," Benny replied as he walked over to the table where the three idols sat and placed the briefcase on the table beside them. "Is it possible to open a window for ventilation, please?" Benny asked.

"There's a window above the main door if one of you gentlemen could oblige," the Fatman asked. Dutch walked over to the door and, stretching up, opened it and quickly returned to the table.

"Do you know anything about gold, Hugo?" I asked.

"Only that it's expensive, Bert, and you?"

"Yes, I think the whole world and his dog knows gold is expensive, but I do know that it's non-magnetic and sinks in water."

"Hmm, very useful, Bert…but come to think of it, my idol *was* lying at the bottom of the cistern."

"Yes, Hugo, like a lump of lead," I smirked.

Benny pressed the catch on the leather flap which secured the briefcase and opening it, took out a small rectangular shaped wooden box, a pair of thick rubber gloves, a rubber apron, a pair of goggles and a face mask, and placed them on the table. Opening the hinged lid of the box he removed from the fitted interior what looked like a round needle nosed file about the size and shape of a pencil and a small glass bottle with an eyedropper-type cap. Benny then put on the apron, pulled the goggles over his eyes and then fitted the half, face-mask, which resembled a bra cup, carefully over his nose and mouth, adjusting it for comfort and then pulled on the rubber gloves, looking quite comical, but no one dared to laugh or smile.

We all stood around the table, leaning forward and fascinated by what was to come. "Can you all move back a little, please," Benny said. "This is dangerous stuff." We all reluctantly took a step back, but our gaze remained glued to what Benny was about to do. He studied the idols for a minute before picking up the first one in line and turned it upside down, then picked up the file and rasped it along the bottom, removing a shaving off the surface of the idol. "This one is gold plated," said Benny through the mask.

"How can you tell?" enquired Hugo.

"See the metal beneath where I have shaved away the gold?" Hugo and the rest of us looked at it like we knew something about metals. "That is copper. This idol is copper with gold plating," Benny declared. He then moved it to one side and picked up the second idol and went through the same ritual as the first and also declared it to be gold plated copper. I stole a glance at the Fatman who just sat there impassively, puffing away on his e-pipe.

Benny then picked up the third and final idol and shaved away a bit of the base with the file before putting it back down. "Please move back a few steps, people, this is half diluted sulphuric acid!" Benny pleaded, as we had crept back towards the table. We all quickly moved back as Benny unscrewed the cap of the bottle and took it off, revealing a pipette-like tube attached to the underneath. Benny then squeezed on the black rubber teat-like bulb of the cap to expel the air and dipped it into the acid and then released the pressure and the acid rose up the tube. Turning the idol upside down Benny squeezed again on the bulb, and a drop of acid fell onto the shaved part of the idol which ran a yellowy-brownish colour. "This one is the solid gold idol, Desmond!" Benny proclaimed, cradling the idol in his hands.

"What would have happened if it wasn't gold?" Hugo enquired again.

"A fizzing, green coloured reaction would have occurred," Benny replied as he began to wipe clean the bottom of the idol and then removed his protective gear. There was a sense of relief in everyone, even the Fatman, and we could all look forward to leaving after Hugo, Dutch and Lorraine had been paid.

Chapter Nineteen

From out of nowhere, Dolores produced a handgun and pointed it straight at Benny's chest. "Put the idol back down on the table, Benny! The rest of you back away and put your hands up nice and high where I can see them," Dolores demanded. The room fell deathly quiet as we all raised our hands. Benny, wide-eyed with terror and with trembling hands, did as he was told and put the idol on the table without any hesitation and backed away with his hands held high in the air like the rest of us.

"She wasn't concealing that gun about her person, Bert."

"Not in that dress she wasn't, Hugo!"

"Oh dear! Oh dear!" the Fatman exclaimed, his face reddening. "What's the meaning of this, Dolores!"

"Consider this my quickie divorce, Desmond darling, and this idol is my alimony," Dolores quickly cut in. The Fatman looked like he was going to explode, but instead he imploded and visibly shrank before my eyes. His mouth flapped up and down, but nothing came out, and he just sat there silently with tears welling up in his eyes.

"Don't turn on the waterworks now, husband, I've had to put up with being your trophy wife, of being pawed by you and your friends in public and putting up with your sexual peccadillos in the bedroom for five long years," Dolores said with a visible shudder and a repulsive look on her otherwise attractive face.

While Dolores was washing their dirty laundry in public, I whispered to Hugo "W-W-J-B-D?"

"What?" Hugo whispered back.

"W-W-J-B-D?" I whispered louder. Hugo just stared at me blankly.

"What are you two whispering about?" Dolores said, walking towards us, gun at the ready.

"I was *trying* to say to my friend here, what would Jack Bauer do?"

"Oh, I get it now, Bert." I shot Hugo a dark look.

"What would Jack Bauer do?" Dolores considered. "I'll tell you what Jack Bauer would do; he'd shoot the lot of you," Dolores mocked, caressing the business end of the gun against my right cheek, the gunmetal feeling cold against my flushed face. "Even you, Mister Shannon," she smirked, the right side of her mouth curling up. When she smiled it had been endearing but now it had become distorted into a malevolent sneer.

"A bit harsh I thought, Bert," commented Hugo, with a look of concern on his normally jovial face. I was just about to reply when there was a sudden, sharp crack of breaking glass as what remained of the skylight rained down in deadly shards onto the stone floor. Everybody looked up in time to see a black figure silhouetted against the blinding glare of the sun plummet from the roof, his 'black cape of justice' flapping above him, retarding his descent. He landed like a cat on the solid floor and then after a heartbeat to regain his composure, raised himself to his full height and strode over towards Dolores, the broken glass crunching like ice under his boots.

"It's Justice Never Sleeps!" Hugo exclaimed.

"Who were you expecting…the Green Cross Man?"

Dolores whirled around at the sound of the breaking glass and in one fluid movement raised her right hand gripping the gun to shoulder height, with her left hand clamped underneath her right to steady her aim, to meet the threat rapidly advancing towards her and closed her eyes as she squeezed the trigger of the gun. A bullet exploded from the end of the barrel, the report reverberating deafeningly around the virtually empty room, and slammed into Justice Never Sleeps' chest with a 'whoomph' at almost point-blank range, and he was jerked violently backwards by the force of the impact, but somehow remained standing with his feet rocking backwards and forwards as if teetering on the edge of a precipice, with his head resting on his chest.

Dolores stood there like a marble statue, her eyes and mouth wide open in shock. Hugo and I looked on in horror, unable to move, but looking at Justice and Dolores in turn, our heads turning left and right like we were at a tennis match watching for Justice to crumple to the floor or Dolores to snap out of her shock. I could feel beads of cold sweat trickling down my spine like a leaky tap and then pooling just below my beltline. Then, to our utter amazement, Justice frenziedly clawed at the Velcro fastening of his tactical vest like he had spilt steaming hot tea down his front, and tearing it open, he gritted his teeth and prised out with his fingers, the deformed bullet head that had embedded itself in the layers of the now holed bulletproof vest he wore underneath. *He would have one hell of a bruise in the morning and would need to go shopping for a new vest*, I thought.

Justice then slowly raised his head, smiled, and like a panther, swiftly advanced towards the still immobile Dolores, then in a blur of movement his right forearm came crashing down hard on Dolores's wrists, knocking the gun out of her still raised hands and sent it skittering across the floor. Dolores shrieked as the force of the blow knocked her off balance and sent her sprawling unladylike onto the floor, losing a shoe in the process. Before she had a chance to recover, Justice strode over to where she had landed and hauled her roughly to her feet, tearing her dress and exposing her tanned right breast, which she quickly covered up.

The gun had come to rest at Dutch's feet, who immediately picked it up and held it with the barrel pointing straight at us and we all again raised our hands. But he quickly applied the safety catch and spun it around by the trigger guard and held it out with the grip pointing towards me. Everybody lowered their hands and gave a sigh of relief. Although it all happened so fast and was all over in a matter of seconds, it also seemed that everyone and everything had moved in slow motion like someone had pressed the 'big red button' that said 'Emergency Use Only' in big red letters, aboard a space station that caused it to stop rotating and create zero gravity.

"You had us all worried there for a moment," I said to Dutch.

"Sorry about that...I wasn't thinking," Dutch said apologetically.

I took the gun from Dutch. It was a Beretta Model 1934; it was light and compact and had been the standard sidearm of the Italian Armed Forces in the Second World War. I rechecked that the safety catch was on then pressed the magazine release catch to remove the magazine from the grip, then pulled back the slider to eject the bullet from the chamber. "Catch!" I called to Hugo as the bullet flew out the side of the gun. Hugo caught the bullet in his cupped hands. "Howzat!" Hugo cried and then threw it into the air and stood there intending to catch it again, but he had thrown it far too hard and it pinged off the roof and rocketed down onto the floor with a clunk.

"Butterfingers," I said, smiling as Hugo picked up the now useless bullet off the floor. I placed the gun, magazine and damaged bullet into my jacket pocket.

From one of his many pouches Justice produced two sets of black plastic handcuffs, which looked like two large interlocked cable ties. The first set he used to bind Dolores' hands together in front of her, and the second set he looped around the first set restraining Dolores, and the other end was looped around the Fatman's scooter tying them both together, much to the disgust of Dolores who attempted to pull herself away but quickly gave up when the plastic bit tighter around her wrists.

Dolores stood there looking thoroughly dejected and what was a short while ago a very attractive looking woman now looked haggard and strained with smudged lipstick and her eyes glistened with tears, causing her mascara to run down her cheeks. Even though she had held us all at gunpoint, I felt sorry for her, so I walked over to the refreshments table to grab one of the metal chairs and picked up her shoe and set them both down beside her, so she could at least sit down with both shoes on whilst tethered to the scooter.

"Thanks," Dolores whispered shakily, but kept her head down.

Chapter Twenty

The sound of scraping and grating noises coming from the front door indicated someone was trying to force entry into the shop. I thought it might be the police in the form of CO19, the Metropolitan Police's elite firearms unit, armed with Heckler and Koch MP5 semi-automatic carbines responding to a report of a gunshot being heard in the premises. Dutch, Hugo and I stood there ready to receive whoever was going to come bursting through the door. The Fatman motored over to join us with Dolores in tow looking very distressed. How he was going to explain away the scene that would greet them was one I was looking forward to.

The door eventually opened, and three men entered the shop. "Lovell, how did you get in?" the Fatman said, looking relieved along with the rest of us.

"I had my own 'key' Desmond."

"You only had to press the buzzer, rather than storming in like the 7th Cavalry!"

"We heard a gunshot and figured you may need our help; I was only thinking of your welfare, Desmond."

"Hmm," the Fatman grunted, unamused, exhaling a cloud of smoke from his e-pipe.

From behind Lovell stepped a man whose face looked like he was in his sixties, but still had what looked like natural brown hair, which was worn long on which he wore a black woollen hat with a row of metal pin badges on the turn-up, one of which was a RAF squadron badge, but I couldn't make out the details. He was about 5' 2", elfin-faced, with a week's worth of beard growth, and walked stiffly like he didn't have any knees, as though his thigh and shin bones had been fused together as one. He was dressed rather shabbily in a light blue shirt with a long brown cardigan, over which was an oversized black jacket with the cuffs turned back, with black trousers which were mainly gathered around his ankles.

"Micky Loveluck, master locksmith amongst other nefarious activities, I might have known."

"Don't get me wrong, Desmond, I-I-I didn't know this place belonged to you," Micky said, holding up his hands, palms forward, which had a bluish tint to them.

"You've crossed me for the last time, Micky."

The Fatman turned away from him and turned his attention to us. "Let me introduce you all to Lovell Schaeffer, an American freelance recovery agent who I have known for more years than I care to remember and who has been tracking the whereabouts of the idol across the globe for many years."

"Hi ya'll… I hope I'm not interrupting anything?" Lovell said, cocking an eyebrow at the sight of Dolores tied to the Fatman's scooter.

"Just a little *contretemps*, Lovell," the Fatman answered brusquely.

Lovell looked tanned and fit, was probably in his mid-fifties with hair the colour of snow, cut in a marine corps 'buzz cut' style and was very smartly dressed in an expensive looking and well-fitting made-to-measure midnight blue suit worn with a crisp white shirt and a lighter blue tie with thin white diagonal stripes. Brown leather shoes with side buckles completed his outfit. He appeared big and brash but was softly spoken with a southern drawl.

"Is it all right to help myself to the food Mister Schaeffer?" said the last of the trio, a big hulk of a man carrying a black holdall.

"Desmond?" Lovell said.

"Yes, help yourself, Tex," the Fatman replied, gesturing towards the table. He didn't need telling twice and strode quickly over to the refreshments table. Tex was almost as wide as he was tall with an unusually large head topped with thinning short grey hair, and had a Lenin looking grey goatee beard, which he constantly stroked. His face had a ruddy complexion which wore an easy smile. He was dressed in a cheap black suit with the beltless trousers being noticeably lighter coloured than the jacket, and a white shirt that cheekily refused to be tucked in at the waist. On each of the three mid digits of each hand he wore large gold coloured rings.

"Do you want anything, Micky?" Lovell asked.

"Err, no thank you, I'm going to go now if there's nothing else, Mister Schaeffer?"

"No, Micky, thank you, I'll be in touch." Micky left straight away muttering to himself.

"Why do they call you Tex?" I said, as he began piling a paper plate high with cereal bars and pots of yoghurt.

"My real name is Brian but, because I like to go to American Muscle Car shows up and down the country wearing a cowboy hat and boots, everyone calls me Tex." *That figures*, I thought to myself. "Are there any pot noodles?" Tex said, while spooning yoghurt into his capacious mouth.

"No, just what's on the table, Tex."

"Has anyone seen Justice?" Hugo asked, looking around the room.

"He was here a second ago," answered Dutch, also looking around the room.

"I think he's done another disappearing act," I said, feeling disappointed with myself for not thanking him sooner for all his assistance today. With Justice gone, I walked over to the Fatman's scooter and cut Dolores free from the scooter but left intact the ties around her hands. Dolores immediately moved away from the Fatman and sat down at the table with the breakfast items on, which Tex was rapidly munching through.

"Who's Justice?" Lovell enquired, as he picked up the golden idol off the other table and gazed at it lovingly and caressed it as though admiring and running his hands over a beautiful woman.

"Just a friend of ours, but he appears to have now left," Hugo replied. As Hugo sat down next to Tex and struck up a conversation with him, I took the opportunity, as the Fatman was alone, to have a private word with him.

"Benny, have you got the certificate of authenticity?" Lovell asked. Benny, still looked shaken from having a gun pointed at him, pulled out a white envelope from the inside pocket of his suit jacket as he walked over to Lovell. From the open envelope he pulled out a piece of paper that had neatly been folded in three and then laid the headed, typewritten piece of paper on the table and flattened it out. He then took out a chromed Parker fountain pen which had the iconic 'arrow' pocket clip from the same pocket and removing the lid, placed it on the end. After a moment to calm his shaking hand, Benny then, with a flourish of bold strokes, added his signature and the date at the bottom in blue ink, and passed it to Lovell together with the envelope.

Lovell took the piece of paper and rapidly scanned through it. Satisfied, he then neatly folded it and put it in the envelope and tucked it away inside his jacket pocket, giving it a reassuring tap on the outside. "I've been looking forward to this moment for over thirty years, tracking it around the world, following up every lead however slim, and now in this shop in London I have fulfilled my destiny!" Lovell proclaimed, continuing to admire the idol.

"Destiny, that's it Hugo!" I exclaimed. "That's the name of the fifth Angel, the French one." Everyone turned around and looked at me puzzled except Hugo. "Private joke," I said to them.

"I knew it would come back to you at some point Bert, nice one!"

Chapter Twenty-One

Lovell looked around the room for Tex who was still feeding his face at the breakfast table. "Tex, the box please!" Lovell shouted over. Tex grudgingly put down his food, picked up the holdall off the floor beside him and walked over to Lovell and set it down on the table next to the golden idol. He then removed the padlock and unzipped it and pulled out what looked like a specially made wooden box for the idol's return voyage to America, which he set down beside the holdall. Unlocking a second padlock on the box, Tex opened the lid and pulled out a large square piece of bubble wrap and a roll of sellotape and laid them both on the table. Lovell reluctantly handed over the idol to Tex, who then placed it carefully on top of the bubble wrap and, wrapping it around the idol, sellotaped the ends down, and then placed it gently into the box which had wooden cradles inside to secure the idol from rolling around inside. He closed the lid and, replacing the padlock, returned the box to the holdall, which was zipped up and again padlocked, before handing the keys to Lovell. Tex then repeatedly tapped his index and middle fingers against his mouth and then left the shop. Lovell silently acknowledged the gesture of Tex popping outside for a cigarette.

"What happens to the idol now, Lovell?" I enquired.

"Well, I've got a mountain of paperwork to complete to get the idol out of England and into America, then I'll fly back to LA and negotiate a finder's fee for the idol, but not to whoever will pay the most for it. The owners always get first refusal, then the insurers and then any other interested parties. After another mountain of paperwork, I will then finally retire somewhere hot with my head held high and my one hundred per cent recovery rate intact. What the buyer then decides to do with the idol after that is their business."

"Jolly dee," I replied.

"So, you never got involved in the Shergar kidnapping?" Hugo said, scratching his head.

"No, I was in Hong Kong at the time chasing a contact who could assist me in the recovery of the so called *Round Table Codex,* which is reputed to document the exploits and quests of the legendary King Arthur and the Knights of the Round Table, which had been stolen from a private collector in Europe. May I ask what's your interest in Shergar?"

"I have a keen interest in unsolved cases like Shergar and also JFK, Jack the Ripper, The Black Dahlia, Paul McCartney etc. It's just a little hobby of mine." I purposefully looked for a flicker of interest in Lovell's face when Hugo mentioned Macca, but nothing registered.

"I did get the chance to read the file though. The kidnappers thought that the kidnapping of a horse would cause less of an outcry than that of a person, but it turned into a media circus. The kidnap itself was inspired and was timed to coincide with the biggest day of the 1983 horse sales calendar when every road in Ireland would be full of horseboxes; one more containing the kidnapped horse would not attract anyone's attention. The kidnappers believed that Shergar was owned solely by the billionaire the Aga Khan who would pay handsomely for the horse's return, but he was part of a syndicate who were prepared only to negotiate for the horse's return and refused to pay the ransom in order to deter future thefts of racehorses. The vet they paid to look after Shergar changed his mind and the kidnappers, who were probably not used to dealing with horses, could not handle the highly-strung nature of a thoroughbred stallion and the restless horse probably panicked and injured itself. Shergar was later killed by machine-gun fire and the body disposed of."

"A truly awful end to a well-loved horse," Hugo said sadly.

"Yes, it was, now I think it's about time you paid these good people, Desmond, if everything is in order?" Lovell instructed.

"Yes, Lovell, it is," the Fatman said as he reached inside his tracksuit jacket and produced three rather thick looking white envelopes and gave one each to Dutch, Lorraine and Hugo. They all opened their envelopes and quickly flicked through the contents, which I assumed was cash, and with smiles all round they tucked the envelopes away about their person carefully.

"That now concludes our business gentleman…and lady, thank you all for coming today and now I am sure you are all eager to leave and spend your money as you see fit," the Fatman said emotionlessly. Lovell added his thanks and then shook our hands warmly and bade us all a safe journey home.

As we all made to leave, I felt a lump in my jacket pocket and realised that I still had the Beretta. I took it out together with the magazine and with my right thumb pushed out each of the five remaining bullets into my left hand as the spring pushed them up, and then pocketed them. I inserted the empty magazine back into the grip and dropped it into the Fatman's lap. "Present for you." The Fatman looked at me in shock, as if I had tossed a hand grenade into his lap with the pin pulled out. "Be seeing you," I said, as we all filed out of the shop.

Chapter Twenty-Two

"Anyone fancy a drink?" Hugo said rubbing his hands together. "There's a pub on the corner," he added. We all nodded in agreement.

"Have one for me," Tex said, as he was still outside enjoying his cigarette.

"We will," I said, and we all shook his hand before saying goodbye.

"For a big man he's got a handshake as limp as a vicar's," Hugo said out of Tex's earshot.

"And clammy," added Lorraine, wiping her right palm with a tissue from her bag. We all laughed as we headed for the pub.

As we walked along the pavement I found a drain along the kerb and fished out the six bullets from my pocket and dropped them into it, watching as they bounced off the metal cover and dropped through the grille with a satisfying plop, except one which I had to nudge in with the side of my shoe.

We crossed over Kennington Road and then came to The Three Stags pub on the corner with Lambeth Road.

"Right, what's everybody having to drink then?" Hugo asked, rubbing his hands together again.

"I'll give you a hand, Hugo," Dutch said.

"Can I have white wine, please?" Lorraine replied.

"I'll have a pint of bitter, thanks, Hugo," I said, as Dutch followed Hugo into the pub, while Lorraine and I sat down at one of the wooden tables outside.

"Why does Hugo call you Bert, Rick?" Lorraine asked.

"It's a long story, but suffice to say he calls most people Bert, or if you're a female, Bertie," I said, smiling.

"Yes, I can imagine it is," replied Lorraine and smiled showing her perfect, gleaming white teeth.

Holding two glasses each, Hugo and Dutch walked over to the table where Lorraine and I sat, distributed the drinks and sat down. "Thanks, Hugo," I said.

"Thank you," Lorraine said poking her tongue out between the 'thank' and the 'you'.

"Cheers!" Hugo bellowed, holding his pint out. The rest of us picked up our drinks and clinked them all together. "Cheers!" we all yelled in unison and took a mouthful of our respective drinks.

"I'd love to be a fly on the wall of the Anderson household tonight," Lorraine said, echoing what we were all already thinking, I guessed. "It would be even better than watching *Celebrity Big Brother*," she went on, smiling along with the rest of us.

"I bet the Fatman just used that shop as a one-off meeting place and by the time they have finished their business today, nobody will ever know they had ever been there," I said.

"More than likely. Where did you say you'd travelled from again?" said Dutch.

"Leicester, we travelled by train yesterday and stayed in a hotel. And you?"

"Basically, the same as you, train from Coventry to Euston and then a hotel last night and tube this morning."

"What about you, Lorraine?" Dutch asked.

"By car from Stevenage this morning. I'm parked in a carpark in Upper Marsh about a ten minutes' walk away."

"How did you meet that Justice character, Rick?" Lorraine enquired.

"Like the Fatman said, we were accosted by two guys after we left a pub last night, and from out of the blue he turned up and sent them packing. Hugo told him of our meeting this morning and asked him to lend a hand if things turned nasty," I replied.

"Dolores would have gotten away with it but for that pesky Justice Never Sleeps!" Hugo added. We all laughed out loud.

"I take it you were in the Parachute Regiment, Dutch, from the tattoo?" I said.

"Yes, I joined up when I was seventeen and joined 3 Para and have been to more countries than I care to remember, and in 2003 I served in Iraq with 16 Air Assault Brigade. Have either of you served in the forces?"

"I served in the RAF for 22 years," I proudly replied.

"The Brylcreem Boys," Dutch teased, and then looked at Hugo.

"No, I haven't," Hugo answered. "The only uniformed organisation I've been in was the Cubs, but I do support service charities like Help for Heroes and those that provide support for servicemen suffering from PTSD, as does Bert."

"That's very commendable," Dutch said genuinely, taking a sip of his lager.

Hugo downed the last of his pint. "It's time we made tracks, Bert," he announced.

"Okay," I said as I finished off my pint.

"We're going to stay for a few more drinks," Dutch said, winking at me.

"Oh right," I said, catching his drift. "It was nice meeting you both."

Hugo and I rose from our seats as did Dutch and Lorraine, and we all shook hands with each other, we both gave Lorraine a hug and a kiss on the cheek, said our goodbyes and wished them a safe journey home, which they both reciprocated, and then we left the pub.

"They make a nice couple, don't you think, Hugo?"

"Yes, I hope it works out for them both. Fancy a trip to the Forbidden Planet, Bert?"

"Yes, why not, Hugo. But first there's a place just around the corner I want you to see."

"What sort of place?"

"You're a big fan of Charles Laughton, aren't you?"

"You know I am."

"Well, it's a place that you can say is connected to him in a roundabout sort of way."

"Lead on, Bert." We turned left into Lambeth Road and walked along the row of houses with bright blue doors until I found number 'One Hundred' which was the only one with the number written in words. Above the door knocker was a brass plate with 'Captain Bligh's House' inscribed on it, and on the wall to the right was a circular 'blue plaque' historical marker. "There you go, Hugo," I said pointing at the plaque. Hugo read out the white wording aloud.

"William Bligh 1754 -1817 Commander of the Bounty lived here. That's brilliant, Bert, thanks," he said, taking a picture of it with his mobile phone.

"I thought you'd like it."

"This is mutiny, Mr Christian," Hugo said, imitating Laughton as Captain Bligh. We both laughed. I pointed at the building a bit further down on the opposite side of the road. "See the building with the large pale green coloured dome?" Hugo nodded unenthusiastically. "That's the Imperial War Museum and just in front of the entrance there are two massive 15-inch battleship guns."

"I'm sure it's all very interesting, Bert, but it would take hours to have a really good look around."

"I wasn't intending for us to visit the museum. I was just pointing it out to you. I must have visited the museum about thirty times anyway." Hugo let out a long whistle.

"C'mon," I said, "let's get to the Forbidden Planet before you wet yourself." Hugo gave me one of his huge 'Big Nims' smiles as we turned back into Kennington Road and walked back to Lambeth North tube station.

Chapter Twenty-Three

We looked at the map of the underground at the station but were none the wiser. "Do you know how to get there, Hugo?"

"No idea… you?"

"I've got a rough idea, I know that it's on Shaftsbury Avenue," I replied as I studied the map for a moment. "I think if we go to Leicester Square, we won't be far off. So, we need to get on the Bakerloo Line to Waterloo then change onto the Northern Line to Leicester Square," I added, as I traced the route with my finger upward along the brown and then black lines. "Then if we return to Leicester Square, we can jump on the Piccadilly Line, which will take us straight to St. Pancras International."

"Sounds good to me, Bert."

I punched Leicester Square into the ticket machine and again it came up with £4.90 to pay. We each fed in a fiver and retrieved our tickets and 10p and went through the ticket barrier and into the lift, and then walked along the corridor, down the steps and onto the Bakerloo Line northbound platform 1 to catch the train to Waterloo.

We travelled the one stop to Waterloo and as we prepared to get off, a female voice announced, "Change here for Northern, Jubilee and Waterloo & City Lines." We followed the signs through a series of left and right turns to the Northern Line northbound platform 1. We could hear the train approaching and jogged the rest of the way to the platform and then walked straight onto the train through the open doors. Hugo spent the journey replacing the hatband on his Fedora from the piano key one for one of black silk with a representation of the four playing card 'aces' fanned out, which when fitted looked as if they were tucked into the left side of the hatband. The train stopped at Embankment and Charing Cross before the female voice announced, "The next station is Leicester Square, change here for Piccadilly Line." We left the train, went up the steps, turned left and right, up the escalator through the ticket barrier and up some more steps before we emerged onto Charing Cross Road.

We crossed over the road and turned left, *hopefully*, I thought, *going in the right direction*. On the right-hand side, it seemed that every other shop was a second-hand bookshop. We walked on and then came into Cambridge Circus where the redbrick Palace Theatre on the right was showing *Harry Potter and the Cursed Child Parts 1 and 2*, and the next turn on the right was, thankfully, Shaftsbury Avenue. Walking along on the right-hand side, we passed an Odeon cinema on the left and then saw a young guy with a mop of black hair and 'Buddy Holly' type glasses coming towards us with a Forbidden Planet logoed plastic carrier bag. "How far up is the shop?" Hugo asked him.

"About fifty metres," the guy replied. Hugo's pace quickened until he saw the 'rocket' logo sign of the shop on the opposite side and he ran across the zebra crossing by the London Theatre Booking Shop to The Forbidden Planet, which was situated at the far end of the crossing.

When I caught up with him, Hugo had his nose pressed flat against the glass, gazing in wonder at all the products on display in the shop window. I must admit it was a fantastic sight to see the *Star Wars* and Marvel figures together with some graphic novels and a 1/12 scale model of Batman's *The Bat* aircraft, which had been reduced from a penny under £800 to under £500. In the other window on the opposite side of the entrance there was a life-size figure from the HALO computer games series which was probably the Master Chief character as well as a selection of other HALO merchandise plus a life-size silver coloured skull and upper torso of a Terminator endoskeleton.

Stepping inside the shop was like stepping back in time and into the present at the same instant, with toys and merchandise from TV shows you enjoyed in childhood to those you enjoy now. On the left was a massive floor-to-ceiling glass cabinet, the shelves of which displayed hundreds of 1/6 scale action figures mainly from *Star Wars* and *Star Trek*, together with Marvel and DC superheroes. The level of detail was fantastic, but they weren't cheap.

I left Hugo drooling over them as I ventured further in. The street level floor was just wall-to-wall stocked with all your favourite cult sci-fi and fantasy action figures ranging from the small three and three-quarter inches to a massive eighteen inches tall, together with toys, mugs, key rings, posters, clothing, diecast vehicles, Lego sets and model kits from *Alien* to the *X-Files*, *Game of Thrones* to *The Walking Dead* with whole sections dedicated to the ever popular Gerry Anderson, *Star Wars* and *Doctor Who* merchandise. I wandered around marvelling at the sheer number of products available and thinking you could spend a fortune in this shop.

Downstairs was where they kept all the books, graphic novels, comics, magazine part-works etc., and was again packed to capacity. I was quite taken aback to see a crime fiction section in the shop under the 'Murder One' banner. Murder One had been a specialist crime bookshop on Charing Cross Road, stocking crime and mystery books plus US imports. It had closed down a number of years ago when the owner had retired and couldn't find a buyer. I had visited the shop several times on my trips to London.

Hugo finally caught up with me holding a remote-control *Star Wars* AT-AT walker. In a quiet corner of the shop Hugo slipped me a thick wad of money. "That's for you, Bert, to say thank you for all your help over the past few days." I must admit, I was expecting some money for accompanying him on the trip, but I was quite taken aback by his generosity as, flicking through the notes before quickly putting them away in my wallet, I guestimated there must have been at least a thousand pounds. I put my wallet away in the jacket pocket with the one remaining working zip. I had no idea what the Fatman had paid Hugo, but I was more than happy with what he gave me, and I held out my hand and we shook hands. "Thank you, Hugo," I said sincerely.

"My pleasure, Bert."

We queued at the till with other like-minded fans with armfuls of merchandise, Hugo with his *Star Wars* AT-AT together with a large Tardis Trash Can and several *Doctor Who* and *Star Wars*: *The Force Awakens* action figures, and I had *The Complete X-Files* book and a pair of Mulder and Scully 'Wacky Wobbler' bobble head figures.

After paying we left the shop with large heavy bags but very pleased with our purchases. Hugo couldn't resist having another long lingering look at the items in the windows before we crossed the road at the zebra crossing and walked back up Shaftsbury Avenue, and then when we reached Cambridge Circus, turned left into Charing Cross Road.

We crossed over Litchfield Street and as I glanced along it I saw a red neon sign displaying Agatha Christie's *The Mousetrap* 64th Year. My interest was aroused because back in 1983 on my honeymoon in London, my new wife Denise and I had gone to see the play. "Let's just go and have a look, Hugo," I said as we walked down the street to

St. Martin's Theatre. "Sixty-four years," I said, "That must mean it began in err…1952," I calculated.

"Wow!" Commented Hugo.

"So, in 1983 it had then been playing for thirty-one years. At the end of the play, the audience are asked not to reveal the identity of the killer."

"Not even to me, Bert?"

"Especially not you, Hugo," I said jokingly.

Chapter Twenty-Four

As we walked back up Litchfield Street I heard a kafuffle behind me and when I turned around, I saw Hugo had collapsed and was sat on the pavement with his back propped up against the black railings, which were backed with sheets of clear Perspex of the flats opposite the Le Beaujolais Wine Bar a few yards away. I quickly ran back to him and knelt down. I had never seen Hugo like this and my first thought was that he had been assaulted or mugged and then I noticed he was sweating heavily and shaking and thought he was having some sort of seizure or going into anaphylactic shock or something. "What's wrong, Hugo?" I yelled.

"Ccc…" Hugo muttered.

"Coffee?" I asked, Hugo shook his head and pointed down the street towards the theatre. I scanned the area he was pointing at but couldn't see anything unusual.

"Take deep breaths," I told him.

Hugo took in a series of deep breaths of air and breathed out noisily.

"Cclo…" Hugo muttered again, still pointing down Litchfield Street.

"Clothing?" I replied and began to loosen his clothing, but Hugo waved me away. I thought hard to try to understand what he was trying to tell me; clot, clogged, clock, clone…

"Ccclown!" Hugo suddenly screamed, interrupting my thought train, still pointing to something in the distance. I stood up and jogged to the end of the street to the theatre and looked in every direction for anyone remotely dressed as a clown, but to no avail. Whoever or whatever had spooked Hugo had now clearly gone, and I jogged back to him.

"He's gone now Hugo," I said, still looking around. Hugo was looking a bit better than he had and I fished out the bottle of water from the netting pocket on the side of his rucksack, removed the top, and gave the bottle to Hugo who took a long slurp and wiping his mouth returned it to me. I wiped the top and took a drink myself, screwed the lid back on and returned it to his rucksack.

"How're you feeling now, Hugo?"

"A lot better now thanks, Bert," he replied but was still looking a bit pale. Hugo was beginning to draw the attention of passers-by as I helped him to his feet and picked up his bags, while he straightened up and dusted himself down. All the time his eyes were nervously darting up and down the street looking for any sign of the elusive clown figure.

"What exactly happened, Hugo?"

"I don't know what made me look back, but as I did I saw a clown walking towards me. "Didn't you see him, Bert?"

"I'm afraid not, what did he look like?"

"A clown, Bert!" Hugo replied with a hint of acerbity in his voice.

"Okay, Hugo, what did *your* clown look like?"

"He had a black bowler hat with a flower sticking out the top, long curly red hair, a white face with a red bulbous nose and a big red smiley mouth, black ill-fitting jacket and trousers with a very large red bow tie and big red shoes." I hadn't seen anyone even slightly fitting Hugo's description of the clown "You don't think he was one of those 'creepy clowns', do you?"

"I didn't get that feeling, Bert, he just looked like an ordinary clown."

"Well, he's clearly gone now, Hugo; let's make our way back to the tube station." Hugo took his bags from me and we continued on up Litchfield Street and then turned left, back into Charing Cross Road.

"Do you mind if I just pop into this bookshop for a minute, Hugo?"

"No, you go ahead, Bert, I'll wait outside."

"Okay, I won't be long, tap on the window if you need me." Hugo waved me away. The shop was called Any Amount of Books and I wanted to see if they had any of The Saint books by Leslie Charteris to add to my collection. I looked through the crime fiction section under 'C' as they had been thoughtfully arranged alphabetically, and managed to find just two paperbacks, *The Saint's Getaway* and '*The Saint and the Templar Treasure*', nestling between Raymond Chandler's *The Long Goodbye* and G.K. Chesterton's *The Complete Father Brown Stories*.

"Are these the only two Leslie Charteris books you have?" I enquired.

"Yes, that's all we have at the moment, I'm afraid," replied the man at the till with long brown hair, wearing a lavender coloured long-sleeved shirt.

"I'll take them," I said, and promptly paid for them and re-joined Hugo outside.

"Any good?" Hugo enquired.

"Yes, I managed to add two more books to my Saint collection," I replied, showing my purchases to Hugo before putting them away in my holdall.

We made our way back to Leicester Square tube station without seeing anymore clowns. We went down the steps and bought our tickets, which not surprisingly again cost £4.90, and went through the ticket barrier and followed the signs for the Piccadilly Line. As we travelled down the long escalator the sound of an electric guitar could be heard playing Dire Straits 'Sultans of Swing'. At the bottom as we walked along the corridor, we saw the young busker strumming his guitar and Hugo threw some coins into his tin. We turned right then left, went down some steps and turned left for the eastbound platform 2 just in time to see the train pull out of the station. We sat down on the metal seats to await the next one.

We were only sat down for a few minutes before the next train came rumbling out of the tunnel and came to a halt. We boarded and found some seats. "What is it about clowns that scare you, Hugo?" I asked.

"I never liked them as a child; I guess it's the exaggerated features they all seem to have, with their big nose, big mouth and big feet. They really frightened me then and they still frighten me now, Bert"

"So, aren't you scared of going into McDonalds in case Ronald McDonald turns up out the blue?"

"I never use the place for that very reason; I normally use Burger King or any other fast food place, and I can't even go to a circus!"

I understood how he felt, but still shook my head. "Anyway, how many thriller writers does it take to change a light bulb?"

"Dunno," Hugo replied after a few moments of thinking about it.

"Two! One to screw it in most of the way and the other to give it a surprise twist at the end!"

Hugo gave out a big hoot of laughter which had been my intention, and I laughed along with him.

There were no Tannoy announcements about the upcoming stations on this train and so we had to look out the window to see each station name in turn as the train came to a stop. After stopping at Covent Garden, Holborn and Russell Square, the train arrived at St. Pancras after about ten minutes, where we got off and walked along the corridor and up the escalator through the ticket barriers to St. Pancras International. Finally, we turned left and followed the signs for the East Midlands Trains platforms 1 – 4.

Chapter Twenty-five

As we were about to enter the shopping arcade, I spotted Dreadlocks and Weasel loitering with intent, leaning against a brick wall to the right of us in the area between the underground and the shopping arcade. I whispered to Hugo to say nothing as we would try and sneak past them so as not to cause any unnecessary trouble. Just as I thought we had gotten away with it, Weasel spotted us and nudged Dreadlocks in the ribs. The two men approached us, but then halted out of reach of us both. Dreadlocks walked like he needed to go to the toilet and Weasel had developed two black eyes and sported a bandage across his nose, and they both wore a pained expression on their faces like the paracetamol had worn off.

"Morning, guys," I said to them both, but they just stood there in silence, maintaining the distance between us. It was like a scene from a Western, two sets of gunfighters facing off against each other in the noonday sun, their eyes shaded by the brim of their ten-gallon hats, each scrutinizing the other's face, looking for that 'tell' that signalled they were about to draw their gun. There were only two things missing, the tumbleweed and the music by Ennio Morricone.

"Okay, Hugo, give them the rucksack," I said in mock resignation. Hugo looked at me and then at Dreadlocks and Weasel, who in turn looked at each other, then looked at Hugo and I and then looked puzzled. Hugo in turn gave a mock sigh and slid the rucksack off his shoulder and held it out in front of him.

"There you go, guys," he said stoically. Dreadlocks and Weasel looked at each other again even more puzzled than before, looked at us, looked around the arcade, probably for Justice Never Sleeps, and then to our utter amazement they walked away as quickly as they could manage. Hugo and I both shook our heads and laughed out loud as we went up the escalator to the upper concourse level to check when the next train was leaving for Leicester.

We walked over to the departures board above the ticket barriers and found out that the next train calling at Leicester was the 15:29 to Loughborough.

"It's now quarter to three, Bert," Hugo said looking at his watch.

"Plenty of time, Hugo, let's have a wander along the concourse."

We strolled along the length of the upper concourse which was named the Grand Terrace with its restored Victorian architecture, passing coffee shops, a mini gastro pub and the ever present W.H. Smith's, when we came to a wooden sandwich board for the Searcys St. Pancras Grand restaurant offering a 3-course set menu with bubbles for £28. "If we'd have had more time, Bert, I would've fancied that," Hugo said.

"And me," I declared. After the board there were three wooden tables with two chairs each side which had the seats and backs covered in red coloured leather. Each table was laid out with four place mats, which each had a knife and fork either side of a white napkin. After that was the restaurant entrance which had, like sentries standing on guard either side a box-shaped planter, each housing what looked like a miniature Christmas tree. On the right-hand side, of the double wooden framed glazed doors stood a wooden easel, which displayed the menu. I looked at the menu and read that the set menu we fancied was only available from 19:00 to 22:00, so we couldn't have taken advantage of it, anyway. On the other side of the entrance was another three tables laid out for dinner.

As the left-hand door of the entrance was open, and out of curiosity, we both went in and peered through the inner glass doors and gazed in amazement at the opulence and Art Deco style *décor* of the interior of the restaurant. It was like stepping back to a time that evoked the romance of the Golden Age of rail travel mixed with the glitz of vintage Hollywood. We then left the restaurant and walked along the length of the stylish and sophisticated open air Searcys Champagne Bar on the left, which seemed to go on forever and was said to be Europe's longest champagne bar.

Walking further on, we came across an oversized bronze statue in tribute to the famous poet, railway enthusiast and former Poet Laureate, Sir John Betjeman who was depicted standing up on an inscribed circular piece of slate, shopping bag in one hand and holding on to his hat with the other while gazing upwards in awe at the grandeur of the station that he helped save from demolition in the 1960s.

At the end of the terrace, we turned left and passed two restaurants with both indoor and outdoor 'on the terrace' seating. Standing underneath the Dent clock was a massive sculpture of a couple in an embrace called *The Meeting Place* but was better known as 'The Lovers'. Craning my neck skyward to look up at the sculpture I thought it had that *Brief Encounter* look about it, and I could not make up my mind if the couple were saying 'hello' after a spell apart or saying 'goodbye' to each other, before spending time apart. It made me stop and think of the countless times I had been waved off and greeted at train stations around the country by loved ones as I travelled to and from the various RAF stations I was based at, both at home and abroad.

Around the base was a sculpted frieze and was inscribed with the name Paul Day, which I guessed was the name of the sculptor, and consisted of a series of scenes depicting the history of the railways and the underground.

One particular scene brought a lump to my throat, depicted on the right-side, soldiers waving goodbye to their families from a train as they journeyed to the Front, presumably to take part in the 'big push'. On the left-side a line of soldiers are shown returning from the Front, by train, their eyes covered with bandages with their left hand resting on the shoulder of the soldier in front of him, casualties of a mustard gas attack and was very reminiscent of the John Singer Sargent painting *Gassed*.

At the very end of the terrace was The Betjeman Arms, which looked like a good old fashioned British pub and served as a further nod to the poet who had saved the station. I had noticed a pointed archway before the pub, which led outside of the station, so on our way back and being naturally nosy, we walked through it to what looked like a road, but looking behind us we were greeted by the red brick frontage of the restored Victorian architectural masterpiece that was the luxurious St. Pancras Renaissance Hotel.

"Wow!" We both exclaimed as we stood there awestruck, gazing up at the spectacular cathedral-like ornate gothic design of the former Midland Grand Hotel, which had been built to add lustre to the station. On the right at the end were the clock tower and the open-air terrace of the Betjeman Arms with its grey parasols, which overlooked the frontage of King's Cross Station and the square, from where I had viewed the clock tower yesterday.

After we had both taken some more photographs on our mobiles of everything of interest we continued back along the terrace and I quickly popped inside Smith's for a newspaper, and then into the AMT coffee shop, which was close enough to the departures board to read the information on our train as it became available. I bought us each a bottle of water, a latte and a ham and cheese panini. As all the seating inside the shop was occupied, we sat outside on the wooden chairs with a three-legged table that had a circular copper top.

There was a supervisor in his regulation dark blue uniform, standing on duty outside the entrance of the East Midlands Trains first-class lounge, checking the tickets of the passengers as they entered. He was tall and wiry with tightly curled white hair, which was almost a perm, and a thin white moustache, and wore rectangular shaped glasses with silver frames.

"Excuse me," I said. "Does the 15:29 go direct to Leicester or does it stop at all stations?"

"You get value for your money on this train," the supervisor said, smiling.

"Thank you," I said, knowing it was the milk train. I turned to Hugo.

"The train stops at all stations."

"*C'est la vie mon ami*," Hugo said with a shrug of his shoulders.

"*Si amico mio.*"

"Isn't that Italian?" Hugo queried, looking at me.

"Just testing," I said looking at the departures signboard between sips of coffee and mouthfuls of panini, waiting for the display to change from 'on time' to 'boarding' so that we could get on the train.

I turned to the sports pages of my newspaper, to check the results of the Austrian Grand Prix. "Yes!" I said, loudly, as I read that Lewis Hamilton had won the race, and had closed the gap to eleven points on championship leader and Mercedes team mate, Nico Rosberg, who came fourth. Joining Hamilton on the podium, were Max Verstappen and Kimi Raikkonen, who came second and third.

The signboard eventually displayed 'boarding' for the Loughborough train and we gathered our belongings together, grabbed our coffees and walked to the ticket barriers, fed in our tickets which opened the barrier and then retrieved them on passing through. As we reached platform 4, I looked at the platform signboard; there were five stations before we reached Leicester – Luton Airport Parkway, Bedford, Wellingborough, Kettering and Market Harborough, and then after Leicester the train carried on to Loughborough.

Satisfied we were on the right platform, we continued walking along the platform passing the first-class carriages, and boarded the train, making our way along the aisle to find some seats with a table which the LCD display above the window showed 'Not Reserved'. We stowed as much of our baggage as we could on the overhead rack and then sat down, Hugo as always facing the direction of travel. At 15:29 exactly the train pulled out of the station as I took a sip of my coffee and relaxed into the seat.

"I was in Tesco the other day looking for any new additions to the James Patterson 'Bookshots' range, when I came across some Ladybird books for grown-ups. Have you seen them?"

"I don't think I have, Bert."

"They have titles like *Dating*, *The Hangover*, *The Student*, and one that might interest you…*The Shed.*"

"Very funny, Bert."

"I couldn't resist that one Hugo. The one I started to read, though, was called *Mindfulness*. I was laughing out loud in Tesco, it was really funny. They are bringing out further titles like *The Zombie Apocalypse* and *The Sickie.*"

"I shall watch out for them, Bert, but I have seen a series of books in the same vein based on Enid Blyton's Famous Five series, like *Five Give Up The Booze*, *Five Forget Mother's Day* and *Five Go Gluten Free.*"

"Yes, everyone seems to be jumping on the parody bandwagon lately, Mills & Boon have a *Modern Girl's Guide to Happy Hour*, Haynes Explains have titles like *Babies* and *Teenagers*, and there is even a Mr Men book called *Mr Mid-Life Crisis*!"

"All tickets and railcards," said a voice from behind. It was another female conductor checking the tickets. She wore the same uniform as the one yesterday, but had long brown hair. Hugo and I gave her our tickets which were again scribbled on in biro and handed back with a thank you that sounded like 'kew'. She then proceeded up the carriage repeating the word 'kew' as she checked and scribbled on each passenger's ticket.

Chapter Twenty-six

Just after we left Wellingborough the sky darkened, and it started to rain. I looked out of the window as the rain hurled itself against the glass and then spent, ran down the window in rivulets and distorted the view of the landscape. As I looked through the window I was transported back to my old job as a car park steward. Whenever it rained I would curtail my patrol and head straight to my small yellow hut and put the kettle on and rather than turn on the radio, I would sit there and prefer to listen to the Morse code-like tip, tip, tapping of the rain on the fibre glass roof and watch in fascination as it bounced off the tarmac and the roofs of cars. The more the sky darkened, the better I liked it. My love of watching the rain went back to my childhood when I would watch it while sitting at the table in the back kitchen of the bungalow we used to live in before moving to the house next door to the Dearlove's. I remember one Wednesday eating sausage sandwiches before going to visit my Nan and I was mesmerised by the falling rain and the two boys who were out playing football in it.

The sound of a train thundering past the windows at full speed in the opposite direction caused me to jump and brought me out of my reverie.

"Do you remember *The Good Old Days*, Bert?"

"How old do you think I am, Hugo? My father always used to say that they called them the good old days, but they were in fact, pretty grim."

"I don't mean the 1930s, Bert, I mean the TV variety show."

"Oh right. Yes, I remember it mainly for the presenter using colourful introductions to welcome the acts onto the stage."

"Versatile virtuosity! Garrulously gregarious!" Hugo bellowed. "Yes, it starred all the household names of the day over a thirty-year period and was chaired by Leonard Sachs. Well, it's repeated on one of the BBC channels on Friday nights."

"Is he any relation to Andrew Sachs?"

"No, Bert, he's not, actually."

"Oh right, I'll keep an eye open for it, thanks."

"Do you fancy a game of Bean Boozled?" Hugo asked.

"What on earth is Bean Boozled?"

"It's a trick or treat challenge game. Each of the eight differently coloured jelly beans has two different flavours, one good and one bad."

"Go on then, seeing as I'm trapped on the train with you," I jested. Hugo smiled, opened the box of jelly beans and poured them onto the table and mixed them up.

"Close your eyes and pick one," said Hugo. I duly closed my eyes and picked one then opened them again.

"Purple," I said.

"That's either chocolate pudding or canned dog food," Hugo said, reading the back of the box and smirking.

"Mmm," I replied, reluctantly popping the bean into my mouth and chewed, thankfully getting a taste of chocolate. "Chocolate pudding," I declared. Hugo then closed his eyes and picked a bean from the pile, it was yellow.

"Rotten egg or buttered popcorn," Hugo read again from the back of the box. I smiled as Hugo popped the bean into his mouth and chewed. "Eurgh!" Hugo groaned, almost choking as he screwed up his eyes and looked like a bulldog chewing a wasp. He then spat out the remains of the jelly bean into a paper napkin and took a long swig from his coffee cup.

"The buttered popcorn not to your liking?" I said, laughing.

"Rotten egg," Hugo said, pulling a face and drinking more coffee.

The game carried on for a few more rounds with me getting hits of lawn clippings and tutti frutti as opposed to lime and stinky socks, while Hugo got baby wipes and peach instead of coconut and vomit.

"Where do you get these things from, Hugo?"

"Mainly off the internet or in shops. Hawkins Bazaar is a good shop for the weird and wonderful, there's one in the Highcross Centre. They even have products from the show *I'm a Celebrity...Get Me Out of Here!* With 'bush tucker' packs containing crickets, mealworms and various other bugs in either chocolate or lollypops."

"Sounds delicious, Hugo," I answered, pulling my face.

"I haven't tried them myself yet, actually," Hugo replied.

After the game Hugo dropped off to sleep. I was feeling tired myself, not physically but mentally, the last few days had had more ups and downs than a roller coaster ride. I thought of reading, but that would have made me feel even more tired and I supposed one of us should remain awake, or we could end up in Loughborough! Instead, I found myself listening to snippets of other passengers' conversations. In the adjacent seats an older man and woman sat opposite each other, I thought they looked more like brother and sister than a couple. "I don't like all those murder and medical shows; life is too short, anyway. I want escapism and feel good factor programs. I must say I'm enjoying the re-run of Goodnight Sweetheart at the moment," the man said, his arms folded across his body.

"I wouldn't share my remote with anybody," the woman replied leaning forward, her elbows resting on the table.

"That's the advantage of being the captain of your own ship," the man responded. Further up on the same side, two women sat side by side. "My friend has just had a baby girl," the brown-haired woman who sat nearest the aisle said as she prepared herself a roll-up cigarette.

"What has she named her?" the blonde with the scraped back hair tied in a ponytail asked.

"Well, I suggested Faith. If I had a baby girl I would call her Faith," brown hair replied.

"I think Grace is a lovely name," ponytail answered back.

I then started to listen to the old chap with the long white hair who was in the seats behind Hugo's head, who was droning on to the white-haired woman sat next to him about the increasing price of coffee beans. I was starting to lose the will to live while Hugo slept on with an occasional smile flickering across his face, when the conductor's voice came over the tannoy "Ladies and gentlemen, this service is now calling at Leicester; please ensure you have all your belongings with you."

Chapter Twenty-Seven

The train pulled into platform 2 of a wet Leicester at 16:46. I tapped Hugo's foot with mine and he woke up with a start. "Leicester, Hugo," I said. He rubbed his eyes and had a stretch before we collected all our bags and got off. Hugo headed straight to the Pumpkin Café shop. Just as he was about to open the red, half glazed door, he stopped abruptly and, as I was following closely behind, I crashed into him forcing him to bang into the door, which caused the occupants inside to look up.

"Quick, Bert, run! Before he sees us!" shouted Hugo, as he started running up the steps. I peeked through the window but couldn't see anything or anybody out of the ordinary, just a few people who had returned to their eating, drinking and reading while waiting for their trains to arrive. "C'mon, Bert, run!" Hugo shouted more desperately.

"It's not another clown, is it?" I replied, as I ran up the steps to join him and, in my haste, I missed a step and fell forward grazing my left knee. "No, it's worse than that, Bert."

"What can be worse than a clown?" I questioned, stopping to rub my knee.

"Tommy Two Shits!" Hugo blurted out.

"Tommy Two Shits!" I said, totally bewildered.

We reached the top of the steps wheezing and coughing and after feeding our tickets into the ticket barrier, Hugo virtually ran into the upper Pumpkin Café shop, sat down on the red leather chairs in the corner and hid himself away, while I headed to the Upper Crust counter to buy the coffees and Danish pastries. I joined Hugo back in the Pumpkin and set the coffees down on the low, square shaped wooden table and sat rubbing my knee.

"So, who is this 'Tommy Two Shits' character then, Hugo, that causes you to run away?"

"You know I don't run away from anyone or anything, Bert."

"Apart from clowns."

"Okay, apart from clowns."

"Apart from clowns and now this character called Tommy Two Shits."

"All right, Bert," Hugo said, holding up his hands. "Apart from clowns and Tommy Two Shits, but he's different. His real name is Hilary Capper but tells everyone his name is 'Steve' as he detests being called Hilary, but everyone referred to him behind his back as Tommy Two Shits because if you've had one shit, he's had two! No matter what you said to him he's been there, done that and got the flamin' T-shirt! If you've been to France, he's been to the USA, if you've been to the USA, he's been twice, if you drive a Ford he's got a BMW, if your house is worth £75,000, his is worth £150,000, if you…"

"Okay, okay, I get the picture, Hugo," I butted in.

"There was just no end to his one-upmanship and he was arrogant and boring with it, and permanently wore a big smug grin that looked as if it had been chiselled into his face like that fellah off the TV who does the consumer shows."

"Yes, I know the one you mean, but I can't think of his name at the moment."

"It's best just to avoid him, full stop, Bert."

"Where do you know him from, then?"

"When I used to work for the council," Hugo replied, sipping his coffee and eating his Danish.

"I think most work places have someone like that."

"Not like this one, Bert, he was *way* too much."

Hugo drained his coffee cup and then looked at his watch. "Half past five, I'm gonna get off now, Bert, as I'm absolutely cream crackered. I'm gonna get a taxi home rather than struggle on the bus with all these bags, order a Chinese, have a few cans and have an early night."

"What you need is some bubble tea."

"Bubble tea?"

"Yeah, it's Taiwanese, I'll take you for a cup next week."

"Okay," Hugo replied, holding his hand over his mouth as he yawned. Are you coming, Bert?"

"No, I'm gonna have another cup of coffee and chill here for a bit."

It had felt a lot longer than just yesterday since we had left Leicester with one thing and another and I was feeling tired myself, but needed to unwind before going home, when I too would order a takeaway meal from the Chinese. I already had four cans of John Smiths waiting for me in the fridge.

"Okay, I'll give you a call through the week. Thanks again, Bert, for all your help."

"My pleasure, Hugo," I sincerely replied, and then we gave each other a man hug and Hugo picked up his bags and began walking towards the exit.

"Oh Hugo," I said, unzipping my holdall and removing the item wrapped in a green towel.

"Yes, Bert?" Hugo said, turning around.

"I thought you might like a souvenir of our adventure."

"Isn't that my green towel?" Hugo asked, as he walked towards me. I waited until he was within touching distance and then I whipped away the towel with a flourish. "Ta da!" I bellowed. Hugo dropped his bags on the floor and did a double take as he stood there looking like he'd been smacked around the face with a wet haddock and was speechless for a change. The tiredness from his deep brown eyes vanished and was replaced by a look of incredulity as he gazed at the golden idol I was holding, his eyes wide with delight.

"How, Bert?" Hugo finally managed to utter.

"Don't worry, it's not the solid gold one, I'm afraid. I had a quiet word with the Fatman while you were yacking to Tex."

"We were discussing the films of Roland Emerich, actually."

"Hmm, very Barry Norman," I remarked. "Anyway, I explained to him that if it wasn't for you having a word with Justice Never Sleeps last night to watch our backs this morning, Dolores would have run off with the golden idol at gunpoint and whatever lucrative deal he had going with Lovell would have gone south. To show his appreciation he gave me one of the gold-plated idols and now I'm giving it to you, Hugo."

"Bert, you are a gentleman and a scholar, and I don't know what else to say except thank you," his voice cracking as his eyes moistened. "It'll take pride of place on one of my bookshelves," Hugo added, as he re-wrapped the idol in the towel and tucked it away carefully inside his rucksack.

"Between the Tardis and the Lego Millennium Falcon?" I remarked.

"I might have to rearrange my entire collection, but the idol will be the centrepiece, and a permanent reminder of our big adventure, Bert," Hugo said, smiling as he came towards me to give me another man hug.

"Ya big softie," I managed to say as Hugo wrapped his powerful arms around me and gave me a hug like a friendly, fully grown, 800-pound grizzly bear would have.

"Bert, it's been epic!" Hugo said, still smiling as he headed out to catch a taxi home.

Chapter Twenty-Eight

The launderette was situated on Nelson Road, in a block of seven shops, sandwiched between a row of semi-detached houses. The block had a convenience store at its centre, which stood proud from the rest of the row, and was flanked on either side by three shops. On the right was a Chinese takeaway, a hairdresser's and a newsagents/off licence, and on the left was another hairdresser's, a launderette and a chip shop, and had its own layby for customers. The white signboard above the glass front door with red painted frame simply said Launderette in red and boasted an 'Ironing Service and Service Wash'. The large windows either side of the door had white frames and in one was a colourful poster for Uncle Sam's Great American Circus.

Inside, the shop had white painted walls which were covered in numerous signs but the sign which particularly caught my eye read 'The launderette is unattended'. *So much for the ironing service and service wash!* I thought. Along the left-hand wall were six washing machines, five standard size and one for large loads. At the back was a locked brown wooden door which I presumed was an office, and two tumble dryers stacked one on top of the other, above which sat a large, square, wooden framed clock, which was always a few minutes fast plus a grey plastic waste bin attached to the wall and along the right-hand wall were a row of six tumble dryers. Wooden topped, metal framed benches sat in front of the washing machines and tumble dryers, low enough to enable the circular glass doors of the machines to be opened.

I nodded and smiled at the woman who sat on a bench with her back to the tumble dryers on the opposite side of the shop, flicking through her mobile phone. She smiled back as I dumped my holdall on top of the washing machine nearest to the front door. She had sandy coloured hair which was grey at the roots that looked like a grey spider in her hair and was dressed in a mauve coloured jacket with toggle fastenings down the front and the cuffs and maroon trousers. A shopping trolley stood by her feet.

I left the launderette and went to the convenience store which had blue window frames and a blue awning that advertised Food & Wines and the National Lottery, to buy a new box of washing powder as I had used up the last box on my previous visit. The washing powders were stacked along the back wall of the shop along with all the other cleaning products and I had to gingerly squeeze between the narrow aisles with shelves either side to reach them. The right-hand shelves were stocked full of biscuits, chocolate bars and bread and the left one had a glass topped frozen food cabinet, then shelves full of tea, coffee, jams and condiments. I picked up a box of washing powder and made my way back to the till, trying to avoid knocking anything onto the floor, to pay for it. I placed the box of Surf 'sunshine lemons & mandarin flowers' on the counter.

"Wash day?" the elderly Sikh shop assistant with the long white beard asked.

"Yes," I replied with a sigh. I didn't have a washing machine in my flat, so I couldn't grumble really.

"£2.49 please." I gave him a fiver as I needed the change for the tumble dryer.

"Thanks," I said as he gave me the change and I returned to the launderette.

I loaded the contents of the black bin bag inside my holdall into the washing machine and closed the door, then poured a generous amount of the washing powder into the receptacle on the top. I then pushed the program selector button to number 1, hot with pre-wash and then fished in my right trouser pocket for some change and fed £2.90 in coins into the slot. The machine started its cycle immediately and the green LCD display showed 31 minutes. I put the bin bag in the waste bin and then left the launderette again and popped next door to the chippy to get some chips. The signboard was red with Nelson Chippy in white and advertised Fish & Chips, Kebabs and Burgers. The red framed windows also displayed the same circus poster.

"Morning," I said, stepping into the shop.

"Morning, Boss, what would you like?" the man behind the counter replied. He was of Mediterranean origin with curly black hair and wore a plain red baseball cap, a white polo-necked shirt from which his chest hair poked out, grey trousers and a red apron.

"A portion of chips, please."

"Open or wrapped?"

"Open thanks."

"£1.90, Boss." I gave him a £2 coin and he gave me 10p change.

"Thank you, Boss, thank you."

I added salt then vinegar to the hot chips and not vinegar then salt like some strange folk, then picked up a wooden fork and left the shop. As it was a nice day I decided to eat my chips outside rather than in the launderette, which I normally did, and crossed the road to the bus shelter from where I had got off the bus earlier and sat down on one of the metal seats and ate my chips using the wooden fork in the sunshine.

The chippy was always very generous with the amount of chips in a portion and I could never eat them all, and after I had had enough I folded the Styrofoam tray in half and threw it in the bin by the bus shelter. I re-crossed the road and went to the Nelson News on the end of the block to get myself a coffee. The shop had a red awning displaying the logo of *The Sun* newspaper and the black framed windows either side of the door were plastered with colour posters, detailing special offers available in the shop. I used to go to the convenience store for a coffee, but in the summer months they replaced the coffee machine with a cold drinks cabinet.

"Large coffee?" the Asian shopkeeper politely asked, but already knew the answer.

"Yes thanks," I said, smiling. I only visited the shop once a fortnight to do my washing, but he knew what I wanted. I had to wait a while for the kettle to boil as he spooned Kenco coffee, which I liked, into a waxed paper cup and then added some milk, he'd also remembered I don't take sugar and didn't ask.

"£1.50," said the shopkeeper placing the cup on the counter. It cost me a small fortune going to the launderette!

Chapter Twenty-Nine

I returned to the launderette with my coffee and the LCD display showed nine minutes washing time left. The woman with the shopping trolley had gone, I noticed, as I sat down on one of the benches and had fully intended to read my Chris Ryan *The Increment* paperback while waiting for my washing to finish but I became fascinated by the two middle-aged women who stood at the tumble dryers opposite with their backs to me. The first woman had short blonde hair and wore a pink sleeveless top with beige knee length beach shorts and black crocs on her feet. The second woman was taller and had shoulder length brown hair and wore a white round necked top with the sleeves pushed up above the elbows and calf length culottes and plastic sandals.

They said nothing to each other but just stood there, although there was an empty bench the length of four tumble dryers available, staring at the tumble dryers as the clothing inside became mixed up in a kaleidoscope of colours as they spun around and around inside the dryer. I imagined the women's eyeballs spinning around in their sockets in time with the rotation of the drums and having a hypnotic effect on them both.

My washing machine finally clicked to a stop and I transferred the wet washing to a tumble dryer next to the two women, fed in two £1 coins which gave me 24 minutes of drying time and returned to the bench to read my book. The beep of a tumble dryer indicating that the money had run out made me look up, it was one of the two lady's dryers that had come to a stop and they were now busy folding their clothing and laying it neatly into a large red plastic basket. The other tumble dryer they were using beeped shortly after and they folded the contents into the same basket and then left.

I felt my mobile phone vibrate before I heard it ring. I dug it out of my jacket pocket and looked at the display, it was Hugo.

"Morning, Hugo," I said.

"Morning, Bert, how are you today?" Hugo replied.

"Good thanks, and you?"

"Do you remember Harry Hargreaves? Oh, you mean the tall bald-headed man? That's him yes, well, last week he was taken home with a hiatus hernia. Well, that's funny, he usually went home on a motor bike!" We both laughed out loud at another one of Hugo's Cissy and Ada sketches and I could picture him pushing up his moobs as he told it. "Yes, I'm okay thank you, Bert. What are you up to?"

"I'm just in the launderette doing my washing."

"Why don't you do it at the one I work at?"

"Because it would entail me getting two buses and then a walk, where with this one I only have to catch one bus and it drops me off directly opposite the launderette."

"Fairy snuff," replied Hugo. "The idol is looking good, as the centrepiece of my collection. I had to reorganise everything mind, but it now sits proud, atop my bookcases."

"That's great. Guess who I bumped into in Wilko's yesterday?"

"No, don't tell me, Bert, let me guess."

"Okay, but I'm only going to give you three guesses."

"Hmm, was it …Keith Harris and Orville?"

"No," I said, smiling.

"Erm… was it…the Village People?"

"No, Hugo, last guess."

"Don't rush me, Bert, was it err…Buzz Aldrin?"

"What, in Wilko's, Hugo? No, it was Julia," I announced.

"The lovely Julia, well, don't keep me in suspenders Bert, and?"

"And, we went to Costa for a coffee and a blueberry muffin and we had a chat and we're going out for a meal on Saturday."

"That's brilliant, Bert! I'm made up for you."

"Morning!" The sprightly grey haired old man almost shouted as he marched into the launderette with a rectangular silver plastic basket with wet clothing inside. He stooped down to feed the clothing into a tumble dryer and then stretched up to put a coin in the slot and the machine came to life. The man sat down on a bench opposite me with his arms and legs crossed and said nothing further. He had a military appearance and bearing to him, and I imagined people still called him 'Major'. He wore an iron grey jacket over a shirt and tie, with light grey trousers, red socks and brown slip-on shoes.

"They sell Blue Moon in Tesco, Hugo. They cost £1.80 for a small bottle, so I bought two."

"Do they taste the same as in the pub?"

"Yeah, I really enjoyed them, but I forgot to get some oranges."

"I will get some next time I'm in Tesco, Bert, thanks."

"Hang on a sec Hugo," I said as I opened the door for a young Asian woman who was carrying a white plastic basket full of clothing with both hands.

"Thanks", she said as she entered and dumped the basket on a bench and fed the clothing into a tumble dryer. Small and petite with long shiny black hair tied in a ponytail she had to stand on the tip of her toes to reach the coin slot to insert the money. I had to smile as she too stood there watching the tumble dryer, her hands resting on the empty basket and her right foot tapping in time with the drum's rotation.

"I'm back," I said. "I just had to open the door for someone. I've booked myself a four-day break in Normandy in September."

"Ooh very nice, Bert," Hugo said in another one of his comical voices.

"Yes, you know I've always wanted to visit Normandy. According to the brochure, on the first day we travel to Caen for a three-night stay and then the next morning we visit Pegasus Bridge and then the British and Canadian landing beaches and finish the day in Arromanches to view what's left of the Mulberry Harbour. On the third day we travel to St. Mere Eglise, where the US paratroopers landed and then head to the US landing beaches. There are also visits to various museums and cemeteries, and then on the fourth day we return home. I'm really looking forward to going."

"Sounds like a really good trip, Bert, make sure you take plenty of photos."

"I certainly will. Do you fancy going to Loughborough this Friday?"

"Yes, Bert I do actually, it'll make a nice change to go somewhere other than the Beaufort Shopping Centre on a Friday."

"Good, I'll introduce you to *The Sock* man."

"I'm not even going to ask, Bert!"

"Okay, I'll see you at the bus stop no later than 09:20 as the bus is at 09:30 and they only run every hour."

"How long's the bus journey?"

"Only forty-five minutes…oh, and Hugo."

"Yes, Bert?"

"It's your turn to buy the cakes!"